A Place No One Should Go

keana-eno-pa-watchee

DL Havlin

Palm Pen Press

Palm Pen Press
ISBN: 978-1-933678-23-8
A Place No One Should Go – 3rd Edition 8/2021
Copyright ©2013 DL Havlin

This novel is a work of fiction. Names, characters, places, and incidents either are the product of the author's imagination or are used fictitiously.

DL Havlin, Author
www.DLHavlin.com
www.DLHavlin.WordPress.com
www.SandySays1.WordPress.com
E-mail: PRLady2016@gmail.com

Dedication

To Babs Brown, dear friend and respected critic.

Acknowledgments and Thanks

I used. to read acknowledgements with little or no appreciation for the author and those cited No more! After my writing journey of the last thirty-one years, I truly know the value of those who vitally contribute to the success of any author on their quest to produce a worthwhile work.

My first major debt is to Babs Brown and Robert Fulton, Ph.D., my patient, skillful, editors/mentors, and to authors Bev Browning and Mary Ann Evans, both mentors whose efforts have immeasurably improved my craft.

I have to thank my readers, past and present, which took the time to critique my work: Chet Collins, Tonya Player, Paul Owen, Judy Galinski, Sandra Pirman, Jeanne Miller, Carol Robb, Gayle Marie Hackbarth-Harting, Todd Sharp, Pat Cole, Marilyn Scarbourgh and Andrew Schickowski combined their criticism with suggestions and encouragement. Their backgrounds include high school principle, teacher, editor, book store owners and managers, lit majors and seminary grad. Aged 28 to 70, they've provided valuable feedback. Comments such as "I hope you understand this for no one else will", "Provide alarm to wake reader when chapter 6 is complete", "Ya-da-da-da-da" and "Bullus shitus", kept me on track, and "Written with heart and conviction", "I cried and I don't do that often", "Wonderful thoughts written in beautiful prose" and "This is twelve on a scale of ten" fired my enthusiasm to write the next page, chapter, and book.

Finally, I reserve my largest, most heart-felt thank you for my loving wife, partner, do-everything assistant…Jeanelle. Without her support, encouragement, understanding, and tolerance I would have abandoned writing long ago.

BOOKS BY D L HAVLIN

A Place No One Should Go

Keana-eno-pa-watchee

DL Havlin

Prologue

A place's past often portends its future. We've heard of the house that brings misfortune to all those that live in it, a stretch of highway that repeatedly claims lives for no apparent reason, or a location like the Bermuda triangle where mysterious tragedies occur again, and again, and again. Why do these sanguine places play host to repeated tortured portraits? Is there an eternal mystic force creating such events in these spots? Is it the knowledge of the past's awful occurrences that suggest new ones? Does a place share a human trait in that its personality and its behavior can be shaped by its past? Is it a combination of all these? As with so many things, know what has happened to know what will.

The following is a letter written by Don Carlos Escavaro, Governor General of New Spain's Florida District. It was sent to Don Pedro Savalas del Tradezo, King Ferdinand's Chancellor of the Iberian Treasury, in 1516. The original document was translated into English from Spanish when a privateer seized the dispatch after capturing, plundering, and sinking the galleon, "Christ is All." The surviving translation, shown here, is the work of the English sea captain.~~~~~

April 18, 1516

To His Excellency, Don Pedro Savalas del Tradezo Written to his Excellency from the galleon, Christie es Todo in the Harbour de Charlotta, Florida, New Spain

Your Excellency,
      It is with a gladdened heart I write of progress made in our quest for the treasures we know are hidden in this en natives has been removed by their own hands. Eparrollik, the primary chief of the Calusa tribe, new world. A great obstacle to our control of the heathens been assassinated by his own people.
      This chief was the most warlike and untrustworthy of the chieftains in the South Florida Golfo de Mexico coastal territory. I have but to relate a meeting with this devil to explain the depth of his evilness.
      Under a flag of truce, Eparrollik invited me and our company to his war camp near the great lake the natives call Okeechobee, he claimed for discussions of peace. Though this is far from the Calusa's coastal villages, I accepted and took my troops, Father Francisco, and his priests. The meeting between all Eparrollik's south

*Florida tribal chiefs and our party was
convened in this remote village. In order to
impress me with the power Eparrollik held over
his people, he proclaimed he would sacrifice one
of his men. The heathen chose a warrior from
those sittin in the conference circle, walked up
behind the man, and savagely crushed the
warrior's skull with a battle axe. This demon
sent for the slain man's woman and raped her in
front of our party and the other warriors. He
finished the revolting act by dispatching her
with his knife. Eparrollik cut off the warrior's
head, telling us to carry it with us and display it
so any Calusa approaching our party would see
and recognize it as a sign insuring safe passage
back to our ship. I'm sure the real reason he
gave me the horrid thing was a warning of what
might befall us if we challenged his rule, for this
Satan of a man told us to leave and to never
come back.*

*On our return to our ship, five men sent
ahead to scout and protect the landing boats
disappeared and were not found. I believe
Eparrollik captured and killed them. His choice
of the inland village was to provide him this
opportunity and to remain out of the shadow of
our galleon's cannon. I am also sure the devil*

was displaying the large number of warriors at his command and demonstrating the difficulty in attacking him so far away from our ships.

Word has reached us today that this evil man was killed by warriors from his tribe who could no longer stomach his atrocities. So in fear of this man were his own people, they dismembered Eparrollik's body and moved it a day's journey from their village. In accord with their religious belief that a person's eternal soul lives in their pupils, they removed his eyes and buried them in a separate location so not even his spirit would be able to find and terrorize them. They described the spot as an isolated mound in the middle of a prairie, where anyone approaching can see Eparrollik's spirit before they get near. The Calusas call it keana-eno-pa-watchee or a place no one should go.

The new chief has asked to discuss trade and peace with Father Francisco. Though the Inquisition has been denied a devil incarnate, Eparrollik's death will be a great aid in controlling the area and searching for its treasure. It is a good day for New Spain and the Throne. I will begin an immediate campaign to bring the heathens under control and to find the riches herein.

Your most humble servant,
Carlos Escavaro
Governor General, Florida, New Spain

* * * * *

The Spanish never found the riches they sought, but the evil didn't stop. New evils were perpetrated by Spaniards, not Eparrollik's successor. Subjugation of the Calusas, whose effort to resist was valiant, bloody, and futile, created a vile page in human history. The Inquisition's thumb print covered the land. But even the inhumane tyranny sponsored by fanatics in the church could not kill as fast as the diseases imported by these "illegal aliens." Gold hungry Dons searched the palm hammocks, pine flats, and oak hills bringing the scourges of small pox, tuberculosis, and other European ills which exterminated an entire race of people.

The disappointed Conquistadors discovered the gold and silver they believed was buried in the land Ponce De Leon called Florida, wasn't there to find. Spaniards thought so little of the sandy peninsula they got rid of it twice; once to the British and later to the United States as parts of treaty settlements. In fact, they were happy to rid themselves of a scrap of land they saw as having no material value. They left little evidence of their occupation except some sturdily constructed forts, cattle that were to multiply into vast herds and form the basis for Florida's earliest economy, and a heritage of evil doing. And, evil is undying.

#####

A Place No One Should Go
Keana-eno-pa-watchee

Chapter   1

The Trip In—

"It's time to get your asses in gear." Ben Callison nodded to his wife and oldest daughter.

Both women obediently took positions next to the family SUV, standing under the bow of one of two canoes sitting on the car's top. Three sets of hands grasp the craft's gunwales.

You have good grips?" Ben's question was more of a command. "We're ready," his wife, Carolyn, said. His daughter lifted her brows and rolled her eyes.

"On three." Ben's fingers whitened as he increased the pressure on the canoe's stern rails.

"One... two... three..." Ben and his "crew" pushed up on the rails, raising the canoe's bottom skyward then walked the canoe off the car's transporter bars. The maneuver was smooth and practiced. It should have been; he and his family made canoe trips and camped regularly, usually twice a month.

Ben's wife and three children didn't have an option for he insisted on the whole family's participation. No exceptions for little league games or teenage dances, specials on TV or shopping trips with a friend. Ben Callison saw this as tradition...inviolate family tradition. His own father had been as adamant in Ben's youth; his sons and daughters made every family outing. Every outing. Just one of many rituals and behavior patterns passed down from father to son, both saw this as symbolic of the control they wished to exercise over their families. Neither would admit that to others and in Ben's case, it was something he wouldn't even admit to himself.

"Let me get a better hold on..." Angela, his teenage girl repositioned her hands as they took a couple of steps away from the car and she assumed a less awkward position at the bow of the craft.

"I've got it," Ben's wife assured. "Ready?" Ben asked.

"Yes," and an "uh-huh," signaled they were. The canoe dropped to shoulder height.

"Okay, go." The three started the short trek to the creek bank, walking slowly, avoiding nature's trip traps, smiling and joking as they went.

"Hurry up, Dad," Danny, his ten-year-old son goaded, "I can't open the back end until you get number two off. I want to fish." He nudged his younger sister, "Let's see how fast we can unpack and get the stuff to the bank."

Melanie made a face at him, but stomped to the SUV's rear to wait for the second canoe to be unloaded.

"You can open the door enough to start getting stuff out. Just don't push it all the way up and scratch it," Ben said.

"Okay," Danny said enthusiastically, swinging the tailgate up and gathering an arm-load. He prodded his sister saying, "Let's go, come on, let's go."

"I can only go as fast as I can," Melanie replied.

"Just settle down," Carolyn said, trying to retain the calm she preferred.

The Callison family didn't show obvious signs they objected to their forced participation in the weekend rituals. Angela, being a teenager, chaffed the most because the trips impinged on her social calendar. Her protests were limited to snide comments. During the baseball season Danny didn't like missing his team's practices, mostly because of flak coming from his coaches and teammates. However, he liked fishing better than baseball. Melanie was young enough to accept the family's plans without question, though she missed her electronic games that Ben wouldn't allow on the excursions. Carolyn, Ben's wife, loved the outdoors, enjoyed the break from home's routine, and the leisure the trips provided after her tasks as camp cook were fulfilled.

All realized that Ben ruled his family in Borg-like fashion, making the axiom "resistance is futile," apply. In fact, the whole family did enjoy camping, canoeing, fishing, photography, and everything else these "back-to-nature" trips offered. It was a way of life for the Callison children who had been on these trips starting as toddlers. Ben saw that his family was well equipped, making them as comfortable as possible while "roughing it." He kept the work load level by assigning each family member his or her own camping responsibilities. Their frequent outings made the whole family very proficient at their outdoor pursuits and the tasks accompanying them.

Danny and Melanie scurried from car to creek over the soft soil and marsh grass that necessitated parking the SUV fifty yards from the creek's bank.

They struggled with camp chairs, cots, stoves, sleeping bags, lanterns, duffle bags, boxes of camping gear, fishing equipment, food, and anything else light enough for ten and eight year olds to lift and carry. The two knew exactly where their father would launch the boats. Carolyn hollered her standard warning each time her children neared the creek bank, "Watch for moccasins."

Running past the adults with his second load, Danny teased, "You guys are slow."

After Carolyn's warning to the young ones on their second trip, Angela said, "Give it a rest, Mom. Don't say anything. Maybe, a snake will bite one, a gator will eat the other, and guess what? They won't pester me anymore."

"Shut up, Bertha Butt," Danny counter-punched.

"That's enough," Ben commanded. He glanced at his pretty fifteen-year-old. She was a stereotypical teenager, though her body and features allowed her to pass for twenty. Certainly, her attitudes toward parents, boys, and siblings reflected those of her age group. She was a good kid, though her preoccupation with her many suitors and her incessant flirting troubled Ben. He wondered how many boys that called and hung around had plans to have sex with her. Most he assumed. Ben's father had encouraged him to "sow some oats" when he was young. Ben reasoned many of Angela's young men had been given similar instruction. It made him over-protective. He told himself he trusted Angela, but not the boys. Ben remembered his thoughts and desires at that age. One peek at her swaying rear confirmed his fears.

When his crew came close to the water, Ben guided the canoe's stern to the creek bank. He barked, "Turn…now." The three flipped the canoe over and slid three-quarters of its length into the water.

Looking at the creek's level, Ben thought the canoe might slide off the bank during loading. Ben grunted, cursed profusely, and resented the time it took to tie the canoe to a bush branch with a line. There wasn't a valid reason for such an emotional response— that was just Ben. True, he had no desire to go swimming in what he knew were February-chilled, snake infested waters, but his reaction to the simple precautionary measure was unwarranted. His caution was a gift from his mother and the stream of profanity was inherited from his dad.

Wife Carolyn frowned. She detested the filth flowing from his mouth, knew she could do nothing to change him, but said, "Ben, the kids. What's all that for?" He glared at her and internalized the heated stream that flowed from his mouth.

Ben, Carolyn, and Angela robotically returned to the car and prepared to unload the second canoe. The three repeated the task unceremoniously. The Callison family could load and unload their vehicle or make and break camp while sleepwalking. A couple of times they did, when bad weather conditions forced them to prove their expertise.

Carolyn saw the children struggling with the heavy coolers. She said, "Danny, those weigh too much for you two. Wait for me to help you."

Ben ignored them as he made his final check to see all the camping gear was out of the Explorer. He locked the SUV out of habit, not necessity. Ben's mother insisted an unlocked door was an invitation to the devil. The SUV's parking place was cloaked by a half-mile of oak woods. Located on fenced, posted, private property, the "trespassers may be shot" sign hanging on the securely locked entrance gate discouraged interlopers. Ben's father would have laughed at him. The tug-of-war for control of Ben's thought process still continued long after his parents were deceased.

Access to this private world near Lake Okeechobee was a perk extended to the three-dozen individuals working for the small Ft. Myers, Florida, company that employed Ben. The 3200 acres were heaven for any outdoors oriented person. A beautiful creek ran through the land that eventually emptied into the big lake. Cypress trees and oak hammocks lined much of the stream. Grassy plains bordered the rest of its banks. These meadows formed marshes in the wet season dividing the wooded areas into land-locked islands.

In places, the creek widened into miniature lakes filled with fish, alligators, turtles, herons, cranes, and water birds. Plantings of millet, sorghum, and gall berries supported large populations of quail and dove inhabiting the pine and palmetto flats. Acorn rich oaks and red gums covered a portion of the property. Turkey, a small deer herd, and an assortment of other game lived under the trees' protective canopy. The property was in pristine natural condition with the exception of the small cultivated bird food plots. Drainage ditches didn't rob the land's moisture so the undisturbed earth kept its plants lush and green most of the year.

Despite the company owner's generosity, the property was seldom used. Most of the firm's employees weren't outdoors people. Those enjoying the land kept its secrets, hoping that the sheet that insured one user at a time would see few signatures.

Ben didn't know of the land's beauty and recreational potential his first three years at the company. The first time he gained access to the property was for a far different purpose. Bill Miller, one of Ben's workmates who shared his fondness for extra-marital affairs told him about it.

"So you've got Suzanne lined up. Have you gotten into that yet?" Bill asked.

"No, I need to find a place. She says she can't get away at night. I can't take her to the local motel. Everybody in that small town would know in an hour."

"Shit, man, you're only a half-hour from the ranch. Reserve the key and take her there."

"You mean the old man's property by the lake?"

"Yes. I've used it several times. Nobody is going to bother you there and the price is right. Take a sleeping bag or a blanket." Miller grinned, "Carry a fishing rod with you. Use it when your other pole isn't in action. There are some big-assed bass in the creek. The ranch is a great place for fishing, hunting, camping, or cheating."

The property served him as an outdoor motel during the brief torrid affair with one of his customers. His liaison with Suzanne was a big mistake and he terminated it within two months. Ben shook his head and muttered, "Damn," at the memory. He visualized Suzanne on her hands and knees, naked, the Florida sun gleaming on her white skin contrasted by the red blanket under her.

Though well-endowed and very willing, the woman was an uninspiring sex partner. Ben considered her lack of animated response as maddening and had confided to his close friends she was as exciting as using a can of Crisco. The affair's vestiges haunted him for ninety days more. Suzanne was hard to shake, for she found Ben's efforts to her liking. Regardless of the fruitless nature of the tryst, the fling provided Ben's introduction to the land's wonders, though he took another six months to venture back for a family camping trip. His conscience forced the delay.

The war between two sets of moral standards bred into him by his parents raged through Ben, though he wasn't consciously aware of the conflict's magnitude.

Taking Carolyn to the scene of his latest indiscretion bothered Ben the first couple trips. He had his mother to thank for that. Her Italian heritage demanded that her children attend Mass without fail. She'd lectured them constantly on the many evils with which the devil would tempt them. This included the sin of infidelity and the need for each of her kids to make a firm commitment to the marriage vows. Salvation through Christ was real to her. Her admonition's always included those teachings and her desire to be able to spend eternity with her children.

His father, an Irishman whose favorite pasttimes were drinking and womanizing, created the battle for young Ben's mind. The elder Callison was quite open in expressing his belief that a man was measured by the number of notches carved on his bedpost. His father's version of the golden rule was, "do unto others, before they do unto you." The pleasures of the flesh and spoils derived from the questionable principles extolled by his father won Ben's allegiance, though not without a major internal struggle that carried over to the present. He couldn't ignore the guilty, dirty feelings that accompanied his frequent affairs and unethical work behavior. They tortured his conscience, but not enough to quit.

Ben's discomfort from using the ranch as his personal bordello faded. He believed his wife knew nothing of the affair, or his many others, and never would. Ben took great pains to hide his indiscretions from Carolyn; he'd seen his mother suffer the indignities caused by his father's behavior who flaunted it in her face. He never forgave his dad for that. However, the property was too much of an outdoor paradise for him to abandon due to some squeamish thoughts. While his presence on the ranch kindled memories that nagged at him—they were easily dismissed; but a bit of conversation, a random thought, caused them to resurface and they had to be "handled" again. He blinked a few times to dismiss the vision of Suzanne.

# # # # #

Chapter   2

Loading the canoes went smoothly and soon the family was rhythmically dipping their paddles into the creek's dark, slow flowing waters. Cool February temperatures meant little material was held in suspension making the water clear. The appearance of "coloration" came from tannic acid, patches of weeds, and dead vegetation covering the bottom. When Ben's family passed over white sandy spots, they could see myriads of fish flitting around beneath their canoes.

A few large cypress trees that survived the early to mid-1900's lumbering, a period which stripped the land's old growth trees, remained, standing as solitary sentinels along the watery path. In places, the trees' lacy green canopy shaded out the winter sun and created a twilight world of cool shadows. Though the sun was close to its noon position, its yearly track remained far enough south that wind breakers and sweaters were needed to keep the family comfortable.

The children, chattering like mocking birds, followed Ben and Carolyn's canoe. The youngsters' craft careened back and forth across the creek like an insane water bug, in spite of Angela's best efforts to keep her siblings serious and the canoe in the stream's center. Ben made sure the adults' boat housed all the critical camping gear that needed to remain dry. Experience taught the Callisons that anything riding in the children's canoe required the protection of double plastic bags. The kids tipped their canoe over too regularly to dismiss the possibility of wet sleeping bags or soggy bread. The erratic course steered by the children's canoe became impossible to ignore.

"Angela, make sure you keep that canoe from tipping over. I don't want to have to fish you all out." Ben felt obligated to say something. "If I have to dry out a bunch of gear I'll beat some butts, too."

"Don't tell me, tell them," Angela returned.

Despite his kids' habit of capsizing their canoe, Ben's mind harbored no serious safety concerns. His savvy children knew the Florida woods, its waters, and its creatures. Both parents realized the greatest dangers were the car trips to and from camping, though Carolyn harbored more concerns. All three young Callisons swam like the creatures living in the creek and the adults knew alligators only stalked boats in bad "B" movies.

Be careful, kids. This isn't the time of year to go swimming." Carolyn kept a parental eye on the children, cautioning them to be sure they didn't get in trouble, reminding them of potential dangers. "Don't bump the overhanging tree limbs, there might be wasp's nests in them," or "Keep the canoe running straight. Don't mess around. I thought I saw some moccasins here last time." Much of her maternal effort went to control Danny, Angela, and Melanie's horseplay, an activity in which they were usually engaged and could get them into trouble.

Ben saw things differently. "Damn it! Cut out the shit! I'm not going to spend half my day straightening out your screw-ups." He didn't believe the children were in any danger; his growls were intended to keep the kids from ruining camping equipment and wasting the adults' time. More honestly, he didn't intend to allow his offspring's behavior to impinge on his pleasure.

Disciplined rhythmic strokes replaced the children's obstinate paddle battle ten minutes into the trip. The "crazy water bug" disappeared and their canoe became the caboose of a two car train running on invisible tracks in the water. Routine replaced the raucous as behavior ingrained by the family's frequent adventures gained control.

Parents and their young ones passed familiar sights: osprey nests, gator slides, herons spearing fish, snakes swimming across the creek, and a multitude of other wildlife scenes notable to the outdoors neophyte, but not to the Callisons. Each got cursory examinations. Only the extraordinary warranted comments or study.

The family approached their usual campsite thirty minutes after pushing away from where they parked the car. Carolyn looked at her watch, said, "We made good time today," and paddled toward the shore as they neared the well-known bit of ground.

"Whoa, Babe. We're going to set up on a different spot. Just keep heading upstream," Ben said.

Carolyn laid the paddle down across the canoe's side rails and looked back at Ben quizzically. "Where are we going? I don't want to camp in that low spot. That place is damp even at this time of year." "No, we're going someplace we've never been before. Since we have a three day weekend, I thought we'd go upstream farther."

Ben "J" stroked with his paddle to keep the canoe moving in a straight line.

Carolyn shrugged her shoulders and resumed paddling. She knew better than to try to change Ben's mind. He would do what he wanted. That was a constant she grudgingly accepted as part of their married life. She asked again, "Where are we going?"

"Up the east fork of the creek. Old Bill Miller told me he used to camp on some spots up there. I want to check them out."

At the mention of Bill Miller's name, Carolyn stiffened, shook her head, but said nothing for several seconds. She robotically continued paddling and didn't look back when she asked, "Isn't that Seminole property?"

"Yes."

# # # # #

Chapter 3

Carolyn shrugged her shoulders, took a disgusted breath, but continued to work the paddle in silence.

Ben ignored her signs of displeasure. He was curious about one camp site that Miller described to him a few days before the man's death. The conversation had been a strange one and was made even more memorable by the man's unusual demise. Ben didn't have to blink to see the remembered image of the incident. They'd been discussing fishing when the subject of the ranch came up. Ben asked, "Bill, you've been going there forever. Are there any other good camping spots?"

Miller said, "Yes and no. There are some good spots, but they're on reservation land."

"Seminole land? Do you camp on it?"

"Yes, that's where we go most of the time." Miller described the campsites, the great fishing in the upper portion of the creek, but then got a strange serious look on his face, one Ben hadn't seen before.

Sweat appeared on the man's forehead. "There is one site up past those I described, through a cypress swamp. It's a beautiful place on a mound in the middle of a prairie. There are big oaks on it and the creek makes a half circle around the high ground. It looks great, but believe me, don't go there!"

Ben saw fear in his workmate's demeanor, something he'd never observed Miller exhibit. Naturally, Ben asked, "Why?"

Instantly, Miller became evasive and avoided giving any kind of cohesive answer. "It's not the kind of place you should go. I should have never…take my word, don't go there."

When Ben pressed his friend for a reason, Bill said, "I'll tell you later, okay. It's hard for me to put it in words. I have a lot of things bothering me right now. Give me a week or two to get this sorted out." The uncomfortable look on Miller's face made Ben decide to not probe further.

Miller didn't live to make his explanation. Within a week, on a dark night, the man fell or jumped out of a fourth story window and broke his neck. There was no evidence to prove whether Miller's plunge was foul play, a freak accident, or suicide. His death remained an unresolved mystery.

"Dad, you missed the camp," Danny yelled, interrupting Ben's musings. The boy waved his paddle back and forth in violent, signal flag movements, causing the canoe to tip from side to side. It came precariously close to turning over.

Melanie squealed and Angela shouted, "Sit still, dumb butt!" "We're not camping there. We're going up the creek branch that goes to the Indian reservation," Ben said.

"Wah-wah-wah-wah-wah!" Danny gave out with a war whoop, dug his canoe paddle in and made an extra hard stroke.

"How much farther is it?" Angela was in one of her whiny modes. She slumped over her idle paddle, disgust shrouding her face. It gave her an excuse to complain, something she really enjoyed.

"I don't know. I've never been there before." Ben's only way to estimate was Miller's comment indicating the recommended sites were two times farther than where the family normally tented. The location Miller said was the best, and the one he warned Ben not to use, the one isolated on the large prairie encircled by cypress swamp was fifteen minutes farther. "Just keep paddling. We'll get there when we get there." He chose to ignore Angela's disgusted snort.

Ben was determined to camp at the new location. He knew old Miller wasn't much on sharing. Ben believed Bill wanted to keep the spot for himself and had spoken before he realized he was compromising his secret "paradise." Well, Miller didn't need that spot now.

#####

Chapter 4

The flotilla continued traveling upstream.
When the canoes arrived at the creek fork, Ben led
them right, toward Seminole Reservation waters.
During the fifteen or more times he'd camped on the
ranch, Ben never explored this branch of the creek.
At most, he'd been around three of its oxbows that
turned back on themselves like a coiling serpent.
He'd never caught many fish there so he considered
time spent on that stretch of waters as wasted. The
stream left his boss's property a short distance from
the fork and flowed from Seminole land.
Trespassing was the primary factor that had
discouraged him from exploring on previous forays.
But Miller's tales of great fishing farther up the
creek and his assurance that the Seminoles didn't
mind people being there if they respected the land
made Ben eager to venture up the stream.

The canoes passed through what was a
cypress swamp in the summer rainy season. They
turned the last creek bend with which Ben was

familiar. The trees grew close together and the leaf canopy shaded out most underbrush. Ben could look far into the recesses of the swamp. Though the terrain was identical to the family's normal haunts, it was a place not visited before and with this newness came a spirit of adventure…and some apprehension. Each bend brought comments about features the canoe's occupants accepted as commonplace around their usual campsite. It also brought opportunities to tease their canoe-mates.

"Look, there's bigfoot!" Danny shouted.

Melanie screamed, much to Danny's delight at his hoax's success. His little sister had a white knuckle grip on the canoe's gunwales. "Where! Where!" She began crying.

"Why did you do that, you little shit?" Angela yelled at Danny, splashing water on him with her paddle. "She'll be up all night."

"Ha-Ha," Danny retorted and returned fire, splashing water onto Angela and Melanie.

"That's enough!" Ben warned. "Melanie, there's no such thing as big-foot, or skunk ape, or the swamp thing. That's all made-up stuff to scare you. The only evil thing in this creek is sitting in the front of your canoe." Ben turned and eye-balled Danny, giving him an angry warning stare. "You keep your mouth shut or you'll get your butt tanned, understand?"

Danny said meekly, "Yes, sir," and resumed paddling.

After a few minutes of silence, the bickering resumed in the rear canoe, but in a very subdued manner.

The family paddled on. Several more twists of the stream brought them to a sign warning, "No Trespassing. This property is owned by the Seminole Nation." The wooden placard was old and weathered, but readable.

"Are we allowed to be here?" Carolyn asked, looking as unsure as she sounded.

"Bill Miller told me about the sign and said not to worry about it. He said he talked to the Indians and it was okay to be in there if you go in by canoe or boat. The Seminoles don't want anybody driving a vehicle in there, because that would open it to everybody. They're worried about people trashing up the place. I can understand that. They told him it was all right to camp if he left things just like he found them. Bill and his wife camped on reservation land a lot. Besides, the creek is public property; no one can own the water in Florida." Ben tried his best to look unconcerned though a shred of doubt nagged him.

"If you say so. It just seems strange they'd put up a sign right on the creek if it was okay to go in by boat." Carolyn looked back at Ben expectantly.

"Paddle," he said.

Carolyn shook her head and resumed stroking.

As if to reassure the Callisons, the creek made two more bends, then opened into a small sunny prairie. The sun's bright rays raised drooping spirits the cypress swamp's dark chill had produced. Sunshine warmed their bodies as well as psyches. The creek widened to form a long, narrow lake, its margins became marshes instead of tree-lined banks. Gators lay scattered about on the pond's surface and grunted in the marsh. Egrets and blue herons perused the shallows looking for small fish, frogs, and insects. Turtle heads dotted the water and an occasional fish struck in the marsh grass showering spray and minnows in its path.

After another quarter mile of paddle strokes, the bank bordering the right side of the creek rose into a sandy ridge. A sparse scattering of large oaks sprawled on this higher ground. The ridge extended to a solid wall comprised of cypress stands and oak woods another 300 yards away. Bill Miller had recommended the spot they were passing as the place that Ben and his family pitch their tents. But, from the same conversation, Ben knew the creek went through the woods ahead and flowed through another prairie. In the middle of that grassland was the site Miller said was a great camping spot and the location he'd warned Ben to avoid. It was a warning Ben had decided to ignore.

Ben reasoned, what could be there? If the spot was infested with snakes, insects, or the other common pests that made it unsuitable, Miller would have been quick to mention them. Besides, a woodsman like Bill wouldn't consider it a "great place," if those were present. Trespassing on reservation lands wasn't the issue because Miller said the Seminoles he'd talked to gave him permission to be there. It was too far away from roads and access points to worry about criminal elements and riff-raff. However, Bill's warning was delivered in a sincere way and exuded genuine fear. Either something scared the hell out of him at the spot or he was a good actor. What was left? A swamp monster? Bigfoot? No way! Ben concluded Miller was faking it to keep the spot the old boy described as nirvana away from others. Ben was determined to take his wife and children there and stake his claim on what had previously been Bill Miller's personal paradise.

"Let's stop and fish." Danny laid his paddle down and reached for his fishing pole.

"Pick up your paddle, maggot," Angela yelled.

"Don't call your brother that," Carolyn snapped. She hated the children's name-calling and bickering. "I don't want a war going on between you kids this weekend, do you hear me?"

Ben heard Danny ignore his mother and mumble something at his sister. Ben turned around in time to see the boy pick up his rod with one hand and make an obscene gesture toward his sister with the other. "Danny, put that pole down and start paddling," Ben said.

"Oh, Dad."

"Don't 'oh Dad' me. Get paddling, now. And, I don't want to hear anything or see any more of what I just saw or I'll tear your butt up when we get camped." Ben's voice carried the serious tone he used when he wanted his children to know his patience was exhausted. He heard Angela laugh and say something in a low tone. "That goes for you, too, Angie," he added. "If you think you're too old, just try me. I'll drop your jeans and blister your ass." The canoe behind became quiet except for little sister Melanie's incessant humming of Row, row, row, your boat.

The slow moving miniature navy reached the oak ridge's end in five minutes. Miller's description of the area the canoes just passed had been very accurate. High, dry, sandy and shady, Bill had recommended the high ground as the campsite for the Callisons. He claimed it was the place he and his wife tented regularly and that he'd only camped at the site where they were headed for once.

Ben thought it was a weird coincidence that he and Bill had their strange talk about camping just four days prior to Miller's death. It was one of the few clues that all wasn't well in the man's life. Many rumors circulated about a probable suicide. Ben saw no sign of Miller's being despondent enough to lead to that conclusion until that day. That was the one strange thing. Sharing notes about outdoor adventures wasn't high on their priority list when they met. Their normal conversation centered on their latest sexual conquests or the next target to become one, or who they'd out-foxed in a business deal. That day, neither sex nor sly maneuvering drew Bill's interest. Miller shied from discussing either. Yes, that was weird, really weird, Ben decided.

Ben would have never considered Bill Miller a candidate for ending his own life. Bill was the office "good humor" man. A quick-minded, silver-tongued ladies' man, he exuded confidence and toughness inside and out. His philandering was an epic open secret around the company. One office wit cracked that Bill's wife should find a good divorce lawyer, buy stock in Trojans, audition for a reality show, remove his jewels, or "check him out permanently." The comment lost its humor when it was suspected Miller jumped out of the fourth floor hotel window—and the office learned his wife had been asking for a divorce. Bill's reason for being in the hotel was that the long-suffering woman kicked him out the day before. No suicide note was found and the door to his room was unlocked, but most people assumed the man made a rash decision and dove to his death. There weren't signs of a struggle or of anyone being in the room with him. The gruesome details of his autopsy disclosed that he'd landed on his face, mutilating his features to the point they were impossible to recognize—his eyes and nose seemingly had disappeared. But, the medical examiner found no traces of foul play and blood testing showed he was sober, practically eliminating the chances of a slip.

What a waste, Ben thought. True, Miller was older, but he was in fine health and had twenty-five good years left in him. The man was foolish. He rubbed his wife's nose in his affairs, doing little to be discreet, much like Ben's father. In the past, much like Ben's mother, Miller's wife seemed to accept her husband's infidelity with stoic indifference, choosing to turn away from the facts rather than face the ugliness of reality. Ben surmised Miller believed his wife wouldn't do anything about his cheating since she lived with it for over thirty years. Ben concluded everyone has his or her limits.

Ben saw this as justification for the precautions he took when he went on one of his trips 'outside the fence'. As far as he knew, he'd never come close to getting caught. He viewed his success with smug satisfaction, complemented himself on his clever subterfuges, and Ben felt he'd protected his wife from being hurt.

# # # # #

Chapter   5

Carolyn said, "I hope it's not too much farther. If the weather turns bad, it'll be a miserable canoe ride back."

Ben grunted without answering her. His thoughts remained on his old workmate. Ben supposed he should feel more sympathy for Bill Miller and remorse for lacking more genuine regret at the man's passing. Bill was the man who had taken a personal interest in him when he joined the company, showing him the methods and tricks it took to sell their products. Miller reminded Ben of his father—both of them had the same outlooks concerning women and ethics. Ben and Bill qualified as "friends" seeking each other's company to swap lurid detailed tales of their latest escapade and, on a couple of occasions, ladies that didn't mind being treated like a trading card. But it was hard for Ben to feel sympathy for an avowed cheater that wasn't smart enough to cover up his indiscretions, or who was so lousy he didn't care about the pain he was causing someone he professed to love. Ben felt above all that.

Carolyn's voice interrupted his musings. "It looks like there are a lot of great spots to camp along here." Her voice was hopeful and suggestive.

"There's an even better spot up ahead…through the next woods. It's supposed to be another quarter to half mile when we reach the wood line." Ben swung his paddle and motioned toward the oaks and cypress ahead. "It's a high spot. Miller told me it was the best site he ever camped on." Ben was careful not to mention the rest of the conversation.

I wish you wouldn't talk about that man. It gives me the creeps." Carolyn let her paddle dangle in the water.

You just didn't like old Bill."

"No, I didn't. He was a real S.O.B." Carolyn stiffened and paddled with an angry, hard stroke.

'Why?" Ben wanted to find out what his wife might know of Miller's escapades.

Carolyn swiveled her head and shoulders around to face Ben. Her eyes flashed with anger and an unaccustomed scowl covered her face. "Fine. He's dead. I'll tell you. Anytime we had a company function the bastard would hit on me. I dreaded going to a party, or a picnic, or even going to the office."

"Bill was a tease. I'm sure he was just trying to get a reaction out of you."

"Really? Would you say calling me at home and asking me to meet him somewhere was teasing? He told me he could fill my tank so well I'd want to come out of my skin. He started to tell me a lot more specific things, but I told him to go to hell and hung up on him." She looked indignant. "Shocked?"

Ben's face showed that he was. "Why didn't you tell me?" Ben felt his anger rise.

"Because it would have been a problem for you at work and because I can handle trash like Bill Miller. Unless he tried to rape me, he'd never get close. And, if he did that, he would have been able to carry his dick around in his pocket." Carolyn looked over Ben's shoulder and made a face. "Quiet. The kids are getting close."

Ben looked back at the children. Their canoe was within fifty feet and all three were watching Carolyn and him intently. He said, "Let's get going," and paddled a little harder to increase the distance between the two canoes to the 150 feet they normally maintained. When Ben looked at Carolyn, she had returned to paddling. He angrily muttered,

"That son of a bitch," after they regained enough distance between the two boats.

Ben tried to clear his mind of the surprise, shock, and anger. He tried, but it wasn't possible. There were questions he wanted to ask Carolyn, but couldn't. His nagging doubts prodded him. Had she told him everything? Had she told the truth? He wanted to ask her, but fear restrained him. His anger made him subconsciously increase the canoe's speed until Carolyn said, "Slow down, I can't keep up." He eased back and looked ahead for something else to focus on.

The creek appeared to vanish at the wood's wall-like edge. Ben hoped a defined creek bed ran through the swamp. Water flowing through cypress heads sometimes spread out, meandering through the trees with no definite stream to follow. It made picking a course to navigate difficult and confusing, particularly the first time through a new location. Ben would have to mark a trail to get in and out. If no clear channel existed, Ben decided he'd change his mind and camp at one of the spots they'd passed. His newly acquired anger made him hope the creek bed cut a clear path all the way through the woods.

Miller, the would-be seducer of his wife, had tried to hoard the hidden spot by trying to scare Ben enough to keep him from visiting it. He set his jaw.

Ben felt camping there was a symbolic thing he could do to get back at the asshole, even though Miller was dead. In a way, it would be like taking something away from Bill that belonged to him.

Ben's eyes focused on the olive-green and gray-brown barrier in front of him. Strong current lines came swirling from behind the trees and turned right at him as they exited the cypress. The creek's significant flow, even in this dry season, told him the stream was spring-fed or that a reservoir emptied into its headwaters. Ben saw the water made a ninety degree bend into the woods. When they were 150 feet from the entrance he could see the creek had cut a clear channel through the trees.

Carolyn skillfully maneuvered the bow around the sharp right turn. Ben worked to keep the stern on its proper path by switching sides and pushing against the water at odd angles to make the turn smoothly. The creek was forty feet wide. Ben breathed a sigh of relief; the banks, though swampy, were clearly defined.

Carolyn looked back to see if the kids were going to be able to negotiate the current as they entered the sharp bend. Angela and Danny handled the canoe like the pros they could be, if they concentrated. "Better watch where we're going,"

Ben snapped. Carolyn sighed, turned her head to survey the stream in front and resumed paddling.

"What's that?" Carolyn pointed her paddle at some objects attached to a huge old cypress standing straight in the boat's path. The tree grew on the outside edge of another sharp bend in the stream, this time turning to the left. Ben looked at the tan and gray lumps. They were animal skulls…four of them. He recognized one as a deer and another as an alligator. The third was the largest and had prominent canine teeth. It was too large and shaped wrong to be a dog. He decided it must be a bear. The last was much smaller with impressive teeth. Ben guessed it was a wildcat. The skulls had been there for a long, long time judging from their appearance and the fact the tree's growth partially embedded them. Beneath the relics were carvings, or what had been carvings. Ben guessed someone inscribed the markings in the cypress at a time dating back to antiquity. The tree's attempts to heal itself and weathering obscured their original nature. Ben peered at the scrapes and slash remnants until he decided the carvings were symbols, not alphabetic characters.

"What is that?" Carolyn repeated.

"I don't know. This is Seminole land. I'd guess it's a religious marker or some kind of ownership sign." Ben sensed uneasiness in Carolyn's voice.

"Those are skulls." The artifacts produced unwelcome thoughts in her mind, fear following close behind. "Do you think that's a warning?"

He felt a little unsure, too, but said, "I don't think so. If I remember correctly, the Indians' religion was based on different animal totems. It's probably what I said it is…a religious marker." Ben didn't want Carolyn bugging him the whole weekend about danger lurking in the shadows where none existed. He knew that some Native Americans had strong connections to animal species, but didn't know if the Seminoles shared this heritage and he certainly didn't know if there was truly any religious connection.

"I thought the Seminoles are Christian, mostly." Carolyn was looking, not paddling.

"I think they are... now. Look at that thing. It's been there for years. The people who put it there probably have been dead fifty, maybe even hundreds of years." Ben spoke to himself as much or more than to his wife.

Carolyn looked over her shoulder so she could see Ben's reaction to the words she was about to utter. "Ben, do you think we ought to be here?"

"Sure. This is a public stream." Ben's attention wasn't on what Carolyn said, it was on potential danger. Their craft was fast approaching the bend's shoreline, the huge old tree, and its cypress knees—projections above and below the water that could turn their canoe over. "Start paddling or we are going to get wet," Ben growled.

Carolyn whipped her head around and worked the paddle feverishly. By the time Ben and Carolyn regained control of the canoe's movement they came within a few feet of hitting the huge tree. Even with their emergency effort, Carolyn's head passed within a paddle's length of the gruesome marker. She involuntarily shied away as she approached. At the point she was closest to the bones, a noise and sudden movement in the bear skull's eye socket froze her. Something zipped out of the opening and over her head. Carolyn screamed and recoiled almost tipping the canoe over. Ben ducked instinctively, but recognized the object was a tiny bird as it cleared his wife's head. From the canoe behind, the children shouted and gasped, frightened and unsure of what had happened to their mother.

"For Pete's sakes, Carolyn. It's just a frigging little wren!" Ben yelled as though she was solely responsible for nearly tipping their craft. The children were talking excitedly and Ben could hear little Melanie screaming, "I want to go home."

"See what you started? They'll be freaked out half the weekend. Damn it!" Ben felt stupid and was mad at his weakness, but took all his anger out on Carolyn.

Carolyn kept looking straight ahead and her paddling maintained a steady rhythm. "I don't think we should be here," she said doggedly.

Though Ben couldn't make out the conversation in the boat behind him, the high pitched excited tones told him he needed to calm the occupants down. "Everything is okay. Your chicken-hearted Mom is scared of a bird that isn't much bigger than your thumb. Settle down back there."

Carolyn mumbled something under her breath he couldn't understand, but his comment had the desired effect on the children. Their voices reduced to a mild buzz and Melanie returned to humming Row your boat.

# # # # #

Chapter   6

After they completed the second sharp turn, the creek straightened out, though a gentle sweeping curve obscured their view fifty yards ahead. Paddling in silence, Ben and Carolyn regained their composure. Carolyn finally said, "Sorry, I about turned us over."

"No problem. I shouldn't have called you chicken. It was kind of scary." Ben acknowledged what was plain to both of them.

"It scared the shit out of me," Carolyn admitted. "I hope that's our disaster for the weekend. We usually have one."

"Probably is," Ben said, "See how peaceful and quiet it is in here?"

Carolyn made a couple of strokes. The only sound was the drip and gurgle the paddles made. Without turning or slowing her strokes she said, "It is quiet. It's so quiet it's spooky."

The canoes traveled another seventy yards, almost around the gentle curve, before Ben and Carolyn could see where the swamp ended and the next grassy prairie started. However, a large cypress had fallen across the creek. Ben surmised a violent storm tore loose one side of the giant old tree's base leaving the other anchored by a tangle of cypress knees and roots that clung to soil beneath the dark waters. The huge trunk was supported by its brethren on the opposite shore. They held its top off the swamp floor and provided four to five feet of clearance between the tree and the creek on the opposite bank. The opening under the fallen cypress formed a triangle with a very acute angle on the side touching the water. Roots that remained attached continued to nourish the fallen sentinel's lacy green leaves. The tree was still very much alive.

"Do you think we can get by that?" Carolyn's meaning was obvious. She hoped for an excuse to turn around.

"One way or the other, we're going through. If we can't get under it, we can pull the canoes over or portage around if we have to." Ben made sure Carolyn realized he was committed to camping on Bill Miller's spot and was discouraging any further complaining. "It looks like we can make it under right next to the bank if there's enough water to float the canoes."

As they came closer, it was apparent they would be able to paddle the canoes beneath the fallen tree. The cypress had been blown over toward the deeper bank. Ben could barely touch bottom when he shoved his paddle down into the water.

"You won't even have to take your bonnet off." Ben referred to Carolyn's floppy brimmed canvas hat, her constant companion when fishing, golfing, or on any occasion she spent time in the sun. Her fair skin and blonde hair demanded protection from the damaging Florida rays. She took her hat off anyway, as though Ben's comment was either a signal to remove it or a gauntlet to be silently picked up in defiance.

Ben and Carolyn came within thirty feet of the fallen log. Ben positioned the canoe close to shore and stuck his paddle into the creek for one last depth check. It penetrated three feet into the water before he hit bottom. "There's still plenty of water to float the boat, but you're going to have to bend low when we go under."

"How am I going to paddle as we go through?" Carolyn looked at the space between the water and the tree dubiously.

"You're not. I'll keep us moving until you clear, then you can pull us on through."

"I don't know. The current's pretty strong here. I'm not sure I'll be a strong enough to get us past the tree." Her doubt, serious doubt, was clearly expressed in her voice.

"If you want to, use the paddle and push on the log to help shove us through. I'll only miss a stroke or two." Ben was sure they wouldn't have any trouble getting past the cypress, but giving Carolyn something to do would make her feel more in control.

Carolyn bent as low as she could when the bow of the canoe started under the tree. There was over a foot of clearance between her back and the fallen cypress. Still concerned, Carolyn reached back blindly with her paddle to push against the tree, while Ben leaned forward to pass under. When his head neared the pile of camping gear stored between them, he heard Carolyn scream and a thud simultaneously. Ben looked up directly into the cat-like pupils of a large water moccasin that landed on one of the duffle bags three feet in front of him. He jerked his head and shoulders up and away from the snake and banged his back into the underside of the tree. The impact pushed the boat out from under the fallen cypress and jarred him forward a little. Hissing, the snake coiled into striking position, while focusing its eyes directly on Ben.

Carolyn shouted warnings to the children between their screams, but her words didn't register in Ben's thoughts. He focused his total attention on the serpent that lay coiled, its upper body raised and forming an "S" in front of him.

"Keep us moving, scull it," Ben shouted at Carolyn. The last thing they needed was to become wedged under the tree with a mad water moccasin in the canoe. She stopped her panicked instructions to the canoe behind and immediately worked the paddle the way Ben had taught her. Carolyn's head was twisted around; her eyes riveted on the snake as she blindly moved the boat forward.

Ben's Smith & Wesson .38 revolver was in a bag lying under the moccasin. It wouldn't do him any good there even though it was loaded with shells filled with #10 snake shot. He resolved never to make that mistake again and quickly looked for other means to subdue the moccasin. The wooden paddle in his hand had a thin handle and would break easily. That would only infuriate the reptile. He looked for another solution as panic nibbled at him. His axe lay on the canoe bottom... near Carolyn's feet. Having her try to kill the 4 ½ foot thick bodied reptile with the axe would only get her bit instead of him. All this went through his mind in the span of a single heart-beat.

Frantically, Ben scanned the area near him between quick glances at the reptile, now frozen in its protective position. The camp shovel, a military surplus variety with a short 14-inch handle, was at his feet. A moccasin could strike up to half its body length. His hands and arms would come in range of the fangs if he attempted to kill the snake with the shovel.

Ben finally saw something that would work. A seven-foot long, wooden handled frog gig lay next to the duffle bag the moccasin was perched on. The tines were tucked back under his canoe seat for safety reasons. He reached down cautiously. The snake adjusted to his movements. The lack of a more aggressive response from this particular species surprised and relieved Ben, for his past experiences with the vile reptile told him any movement normally elicited an attack. Ben eased the handle toward him, then up. When the pole reached the top of the bag, the moccasin struck. Its white mouth slashed forward and Ben could feel the impact transmitted up the wood. The snake recoiled into striking position.

Ben whipped the gig around and without hesitation drove the tines into the snake right behind the head. The reptile coiled and writhed around the pole desperately trying to dislodge the pain that afflicted it. Ben quickly lifted the impaled moccasin out of the boat and submerged it in the water. The cracking sound the handle made as he hoisted the heavy snake from the canoe startled him, but it held together as he attempted to drown the serpent.

For the first time since the snake dropped into the boat, Ben was aware of what was happening outside of the five foot area of focus in front of him. The children already had paddled their canoe under the tree and watched, wide-eyed and awestruck, as the battle between their father and the moccasin played out. Carolyn, shaking and crying, faced Ben, her body contorted around in the front seat. "Keep us moving," Ben said softly.

Carolyn nodded, faced forward, and paddled toward the swamp's opening to the prairie, now only twenty yards away. He heard Angela's and Danny's questions and Melanie's pleas to go home. Ben dismissed their prattle with a curt remark telling the children, "Quiet down. We'll discuss the whole thing after we make camp."

The throbbing gig handle transmitted the snake's movements as it struggled to free itself. After a few minutes that seemed an hour, the pole became still. Ben brought the snake close to the surface and watched it to be sure it was dead. Its body trailed the pole lifelessly, its only movement created by Carolyn's paddling. After a minute more he lifted the moccasin from the water and said triumphantly, "That's one slithering bastard that won't bother anybody again."

Danny and the girls cheered as he shook the gig pole to dislodge the snake from the tines. The weight and strain were too much for the cracked handle and it broke a few inches above the gig. Slowly, the snake with the steel tines still imbedded, disappeared into the creek waters.

Ben picked up his paddle and resumed stroking. "Well, now our weekend disaster is over. We can enjoy the rest of the trip."

"We shouldn't be here," Carolyn reiterated.

"Bull shit."

"We shouldn't be here." Carolyn kept paddling.

# # # # #

Chapter 7

At the Place

Ben recognized the campsite immediately. Bill Miller's description was very accurate and the isolated nature of the location left no doubt. The small round mound sat in the middle of the prairie. Their canoes approached on the creek which made an oxbow enclosing most of the hillock. Gentle flowing water created a moat on 300degrees of the site's circumference. Past the campsite, the creek continued to another swamp several hundred yards away. Oak woods and cypress heads surrounded the vast dry marsh. Ben thought the terrain must look unique from the air; a self-contained island world floating in a universe of long green grass. The forest, enclosing the prairie on all sides with its solid barrier of timber and leaves, gave the impression of prison walls. Five large live oaks grew on the mound, the only large trees growing on the plain. Their limbs sprawled out, low to the ground, providing a wealth of places for the kids to climb. There was something strange about the oaks, but Ben couldn't figure out what it was.

The mound was thirty yards in diameter and stood seven feet higher than its surroundings. It was a perfect place to camp. Dry, with level land to pitch the tents, plenty of shade, a plethora of firewood, and little or no weeds even away from under the oaks, it provided everything an outdoors-person could want in a rustic site.

Ben slowly realized the little hill they were about to camp on shouldn't be there. Not naturally. He didn't believe there was enough current in the small creek to have deposited so much soil in that particular location. And, if the spot was an alluvial deposit, there certainly wasn't anything to have caused earth to be piled so high. The mound must have been made by man. It hadn't been created recently. The girth of the oaks growing on the earthen hump provided evidence of its antiquity, probably 150 years, maybe many more.

Ben surveyed the site. It looked like some of the mounds and mittens he'd seen on the Gulf Coast at the Randell Research Center, an archeological site that studied the Calusa Indian tribe, or at Hontoon State Park located farther north in the center of the state, that featured mounds built by another tribe, the Timucuans. The humps of earth had served several purposes for the natives. Often starting as trash heaps, they served as sites for ceremonies, burial, defense, and elevated living space. His family was about to pitch their tents on an Indian mound, Ben was sure of it. In this part of Florida, it was probably the Calusas or an off-shoot tribe that had built a small family village on this oasis in the marsh grass dessert more than a thousand years ago.

Ben's first inclination was to impress Carolyn and his kids with his deductions regarding their new campground. The words were forming in his brain when another thought caused him to remain silent. If he told his family the spot was probably an Indian mound, their imaginations might run wild. The kids would invent a scary history for the place that never occurred. Carolyn would likely conclude they were on an archeological site that shouldn't be disturbed or maybe she'd fear it was a burial ground. Horror movies would come to her mind. He'd be calming a panicked wife and scared children all weekend. It was best if he kept his opinion to himself, though his bragging side protested his silence. As he approached the campsite, nosing the canoe through the narrow band of lily pads ringing the mound and finding a good spot to unload commanded his attention. All thoughts of the place's history evaporated as he concentrated.

Ben could see the bottom, stuck the paddle down to the sand, confirming the depth was less than a foot. Using the paddle to stabilize the canoe, he swung his feet over the rails.

"Okay, let's get this done," Ben said as he splashed into the creek, barely rocking the canoe.

"I want to go fishing," Danny shouted.

"Not until the gear's unloaded, the tents are pitched, and the kitchen's set up," Ben reached his hand out to Carolyn to help her balance as she got out of the aluminum hull. "The faster it gets done, the faster we go fishing."

Unloading the canoes took fifteen minutes of family effort, though trying to keep Melanie and Danny busy wasn't easy. Ben stood in shin deep water next to the canoes, lifting and handing gear to Carolyn who passed it to the children. The three kids scurried back and forth to the middle of the sandy hump, piling the equipment under one of the huge old oaks. They were easily distracted by things like the sound of quail whistling in the meadow or osprey riding the wind currents above. He'd remind them to get back on task by saying, "What are you doing?"

When Ben removed the splintered gig pole from the canoe he examined the mangled wood that had been located a few inches above the missing steel tines. He shuddered involuntarily. A cold feeling invaded him as he touched the wood shards the moccasin had coiled around as it fought for its life. The hair on his neck raised—biblical stories remembered from his youth subconsciously connected evil with serpents and he abhorred the slithering creatures.

"That scared the poop out of me. I wanted to jump out of the canoe. I'm glad you stayed so cool," Carolyn said.

"It sure got my attention. I'm glad I didn't drink too much coffee this morning. I'd be changing shorts right now if I had." His eyes searched the mound. "There isn't much brush cover under the oaks. It's almost like this place has been cleared off. It sure is unusual, but that's good. I don't think we have to worry about the kids getting snake bit." Ben saw the question in his wife's eyes. He sighed and said, "The moccasin? I'd prefer not to make a big thing about what happened this morning. I don't want them scared shitless all weekend."

"I guess I agree." She squinted at him through sunlight reflecting off the creek waters. Carolyn hunched her shoulders and frowned, "This place kind of gives me a creepy feeling."

"It's just new. Think about it, it's not very different from our old campsite. You'll get over it. In a few hours…" Ben moved his hand not holding the shattered gig upward, "Poof, that feeling will be gone." He examined the splintered handle one more time before tossing it disgustedly back into the canoe. "I won't be doing any frog gigging, I guess."

* * *

It didn't take long for the family to set up camp. Tents were soon pitched, sleeping gear stored inside, the camp kitchen erected, and a campfire site selected. Carolyn made sandwiches while Ben, Melanie, Danny and Angela completed finishing touches on the camp. The site had no evidence of any recent human visitation. Bill Miller had been there within sixty days. At least the bastard did a good job of cleaning up the site after his only visit.

The family crawled back into their canoes shortly after lunch. Unexpectedly, Carolyn decided to join them. On most trips, she spent her days reclining in a camp lounger, alternately reading and snoozing in the sun. Ben couldn't tell if her reason for accompanying them came from a desire to explore the new territory or a desire to avoid being in the new campsite alone. She'd been quieter than usual when they put up the tent and stowed their gear. Ben wondered if their experiences in the morning or the fact they trespassed on the Indians' reservation continued to frighten her, but he refused to ask and give Carolyn an opportunity to suggest leaving. Ben decided they were settled and they were going to stay.

# # # # #

Chapter   8

"I have another one," Melanie squealed as she hoisted another speckled perch into the kid's canoe. The fish flopped around on its aluminum floor. "Take it off the hook for me, Angela," she pleaded. The twelve-inch fish looked like it had been made with the same cookie-cutter as the twenty plus perch they'd already caught.

"Swing it back here," Angela said.
Melanie lifted her cane pole, whipped the "speck" off the floor, and whapped Danny in the back of the head with the wriggling fish. The perch hung over the bow briefly before Melanie swung the fish into Angela's face who sat in the stern.

"Watch what you're doing, dork!" Danny warned.

"Sssppppfffttt," Angela spit as she groped for the line. "You're going to have to learn to do this yourself." Angela backed the hook out of the fish's mouth.

"Sorry," Melanie said, but her giggle abridged its sincerity. "I guess you want me to bait your hook, too."

"Uh-huh, please." Melanie waited patiently for Angela to scoop a minnow out of the bucket.

The fishing was as good as Bill Miller said, Ben conceded grudgingly. At least the asshole hadn't lied about that. He watched Angela place the fish into a large metal mesh bag full of speckled perch, bluegill, and even a couple catfish the children caught on their minnows and worms. Ben and Carolyn caught bass throughout the afternoon, including one large fish weighing over seven pounds. The fish bit so well even his wife kept her rod in hand longer than usual. Thoughts of the eerie marker, the brush with the snake, Bill Miller, and every other trouble disappeared from Ben's mind, except when Carolyn made a comment or two about her concerns about trespassing. He wasn't sure of Carolyn's comfort level, but she would have to deal with it. Ben led the family back to the campsite after three hours in the canoes.

* * *

"Let me get my camera," Carolyn said. She always took pictures of their catch and this was an exceptional one. Ben laid the bass, specks, catfish, and bluegills they'd elected to keep out on a patch of grass. It was enough for several meals.

Carolyn snapped pictures as Ben cleaned the fish for their ritual camp dinner. The children, still enthused from the afternoon trip, fished from the shore, but their efforts went un-rewarded. The excellent fishing on either segment of the creek to or from the campsite was non-existent in the waters bending around the mound.

Angela noticed something else. It wasn't only fish that seemed to be missing from the spot. No turtles, frogs, gators, birds, snakes, not even lizards scurried around the earth on the mound or moved through the oak trees. She asked her father, "No wildlife lives on this mound. Have any idea why?"

Ben said, "I hadn't noticed, but what the Hell, that's an advantage. Think about it. After our ordeal with the water moccasin this morning, it just adds to this site's appeal." Ben tried to blow her comment off, but though his words showed no concern, a seed was planted—the lack of nature's creatures nagged at him. That was very strange.

The family gathered firewood and stacked it for the evening campfire. Ben had selected a spot for an inferno—he preferred large blazes. He chose an open spot in the midst of the oaks, one with no leaves or Spanish moss above it to catch fire, and forty feet away from their tents and coolers. The fire would help keep raccoons and other night marauding four-legged critters away while they were sleeping, if they showed up at this place that was so unpopular with animals. Problem was, a big fire might attract two-legged pests in the form of humans which were far more dangerous. The land was Indian reservation. If the Seminoles saw the campfire, it was logical to assume they'd investigate, and Carolyn's words, "We shouldn't be here," wouldn't exit his thoughts. Those concerns prompted his next action.

Ben entered the tent and removed his gun from a knapsack. He removed the shells containing snake shot and reloaded his .38caliber revolver with bullets. After vacantly staring at the weapon for a minute, he decided to make its new night-time residence the cot under his sleeping bag. The coming darkness might bring surprises. If animals raiding the camp became too much of a nuisance, he'd probably have to kill a couple. That usually discouraged the rest. Ben told himself he didn't like killing the varmints, but it sometimes became a necessity to keep the raccoons, possums, and pigs from damaging camping gear and disturbing his family's sleep. He purposely tried dismissing speculation about shooting another human, but couldn't. It would be difficult, but he believed he could if his family or he was threatened.

He was sure the safety was on before he slid the gun under his bag. Ben remembered his father had spoken casually about his Vietnam experience. He'd assured Ben that, "It was easy to kill, if you knew the other guy wanted to kill you." Ben's mother had done all she could to counter that argument. She preached non-violence. "How can you tell what's in another man's mind? Remember, you're being watched every second. Do you want to face God knowing that you've violated his laws?" Ben was conflicted every time he touched his weapon. An uncomfortable feeling rolled over him like a cold wave as he exited the tent. For some reason, intuition told him he should take the gun with him.

# # # # #

Chapter   9

"No burnt faces or arms." Carolyn held a bottle up and shook it. "The sun is as strong here as it is in the boats."

Danny and Melanie grumbled but crept over to their mother. "The sun's not that strong now," Angela whined.

"It's strong enough." Carolyn motioned for her daughter to come.

"I want to get a tan, Mom," Angela grumbled.

"You'll tan some under this stuff," Carolyn said and removed the cap.

"Awwww, Mom," Angela complained as she came for her final coat of the day.

Carolyn's insistence everyone apply another coat of sunscreen was indicative of her constant concern for her children. It took time to smear the cream on the protesting young ones and it was late in the day. But Carolyn knew she wouldn't feel guilty if one of her kids developed skin cancer later in life. All the little things she did were worth knowing that she'd done her parental best to protect them.

Angela lobbied for her father to erect canvas around the latrine dug earlier. The openness of the site didn't afford her the privacy she wanted. He did that grudgingly. Ben grumbled as time slipped away. The sun was accelerating its race to the horizon. He wanted a fire pit dug, the logs cut and piled neatly, wood arranged in wigwam fashion to start the blaze, and all potential combustible vegetation cleared around its circumference before sundown. Time was fleeting and Carolyn and he concentrated on that final camp formality.

As Ben and Carolyn were bent over, absorbed in preparing the fire site, a voice called out, "Hello." In surprise, Ben glanced up. It came from a man who stood on the creek's opposite shoreline. An Indian by appearance, he was medium height with a muscular stocky build, his form strikingly silhouetted against the greens, tans, and yellows of the prairie grasses growing behind him. His bare head housed a full crop of neatly combed, medium length, jet-black hair. Copper-brown skin accented the whites of his eyes and their deep brown iris. The Indian wore a red and gray plaid flannel shirt, a red bandana around his neck, jeans, and boots.

"Hello," Ben answered. He wished he'd bowed to his intuition and had his revolver in his pocket.

"Did you catch many fish today?" the stranger asked in a friendly tone.

"We did all right." Ben's answer was as non-specific as he could make it. He had no intention of revealing how many fish they took.

"This is a good place to fish. The big bass are near that swamp." The man pointed downstream toward the cypress. "Be careful, there are many snakes there."

Ben straightened up and took a couple steps toward their visitor. There was something strange about the man's speech pattern, though his English was perfect. He felt Carolyn's hand on his arm, stopping him. "We found out about the snakes this morning."

"Humph." The man nodded his head. "This time of year they lay in the sun to warm themselves. If they get too warm, they crawl under something. It is then they are most dangerous. Be careful where you walk and put your hands and you will be all right."

"Is it all right for us to be here?" Carolyn asked.

The Indian hesitated for a second, "To fish? No one minds as long as you come by canoe or boat. The elders do not want anyone to drive vehicles in here."

"Is it all right to camp on reservation land?" Carolyn persisted.

Ben gave her a dirty look.

The man remained silent for several seconds before saying anything. It was apparent the Indian was phrasing his answer carefully. "I do not care. Most of the people would say nothing to you. Do not be destructive to Mother Earth and I do not believe anyone will object. Take only the fish and game you can use and no one will tell you to go." He hesitated then added, "You are going to camp here?" He pointed to the tents.

Ben nodded, "You can see we're already set up. It's a great spot."

The Indian folded his arms. "This spot is not a good place for you. You should find another.

Ben asked, "Why?"

"You would think I am superstitious and ignorant if I told you and you would not believe me. There are many good sites in either direction. You passed some when you came in. There are more past the cypress upstream. It will be better for you if you use one of them."

"Are the snakes bad here, or mosquitoes, or what?" Ben asked. "No."

"Then what makes it a bad spot?" Ben persisted.

"It is a very bad place." The Indian wasn't going to willingly tell the mound's secret.

"Are we in danger now?" Carolyn's voice became shrill with alarm.

"No lady, only after dark." The Indian rocked back and forth on his heels a little bit.

"We saw a marker coming up the creek, skulls and some other stuff. Is that to keep people out?" Ben wondered why the man wanted them to leave where they were and immediately speculated on reasons. The prairie would make an ideal spot for a drug drop. It was a possibility. Ben's imagination searched for alternatives. Maybe the Indian didn't want them to find something. That was it, he concluded, there was something hidden around or in the mound.

Carolyn asked, "Where do you think we..."

Ben interrupted Carolyn's question by shaking his head and saying, "I'm sure there's a reason you think we should move. I'd be interested in what it is."

The Indian stood in silence as he looked at Ben intently. No malice, anger, or urgency showed in the man's eyes. He was taking Ben's measure. Finally, he decided. The Indian nodded, opened his arms and extended his hands, palms upward, in a gesture of frank ness as he began to speak. "I am an educated person. I have a degree in mechanical engineering from Georgia Tech. I tell you this so you can place a value on what I say." The man refolded his arms. "This place is very ancient. The old ones, the Calusa, they who lived here before the Seminole, called it 'Keana-eno-pa-watchee' in their language. In English it means, 'a place no one should go.' The ground you stand on is evil. Some of our medicine men did not believe. They came here—then they believed. More years ago than can be counted, the chiefs decided no one should come to this place. That is what the marker means. Only the totems of the snake and the panther can walk here and then only in the day."

"Why are you here?" Ben asked.

"I am the sign of the snake. No one else comes here and I like to be alone at times. But, I am gone before the night."

"You said its evil here. Do you know why?" Ben asked. "Only the old story you will not believe."

Carolyn motioned toward the children who had stopped their activities and were listening to the conversation. "No, Ben," she said.

"Tell me. I'd like to hear it." Ben ignored Carolyn's warning.

The Indian shrugged his shoulders and said, "The old ones had a wicked chief. He killed at his whim and took women from the tribe's men. The tribe eventually rebelled against his murders and rapes and they killed him. But, the evil one came back from his grave and terrorized the village at night. The story is that they brought his body here, cut it in many pieces, and made the mound over the parts of his body so he could not get out. The Calusa believed a person's spirits lived in their shadow, their reflection in water, and in the pupil of their eye. After death, the shadow and reflection spirits disappeared, but the old ones said the spirit in the eye was immortal. For this reason, they removed the evil chief's eyes and hid them far away, so he could not find the rest of his corpse. They believed his spirit would search for his body, then find them each night and seek revenge. But, this place was far from their village. Farther than a man or spirit could walk in a day and a night. Only if they came here at night did the evil spirit bother them. Even so, that is when they named this spot, Keana-eno-pa-watchee. It is said only the purest of heart, those with no evil in them, are free to come here. The evil one gets stronger by seizing others who have bad hearts."

"Do you leave before dark because you're afraid there's evil in you?" Ben asked pointedly.

"I am unwilling to find out," the Indian answered.

"That's a hell of a story." Ben purposely emphasized the word story.

"You asked, so I told you." The Indian answered without rancor or change of expression.

Ben realized his remarks pushed past propriety. He was a guest on the Indians' land and the man hadn't been threatening. Ben saw the story as a clever device, one designed to convince his family and him to move on their own accord. He didn't know the man's motives, but Ben was sure there were some. "No disrespect intended. I'm sorry, it's just difficult for me to understand and identify with parts of your culture. I don't mean to offend you."

The Indian nodded.

Ben tried to read the Indian's features, but they told him nothing. Ben asked, "Are you asking us to leave this place?"

"No. The decision is for you to make."

"Would you like some fish?" Ben changed the subject and made a peace offering. "We have plenty."

"Thank you for your offer, but I don't eat... fish."

"If you want some for your friends or for yourself, we'll be here," Ben said, his answer indicating his intention of staying.

The Indian remained silent for several seconds. His expression didn't change. At last he unfolded his arms and said, "I wish good fishing for you and good luck." He held his hand up, then turned and walked toward the distant woods. His unspoken message was, "I warned you."

Carolyn maintained a stranglehold on Ben's arm as the Indian strode across the prairie. When she knew the man couldn't hear, she said, "We aren't going to stay here, are we?"

"You didn't believe that bull shit, did you?"

"The part about an evil spirit being here…no. The fact he wanted us off this spot, yes."

"He's not going to do anything. He just wanted to scare the shit out of the palefaces." Ben sounded sure of himself…more than he actually was.

"If his intent was to scare me, it worked," Carolyn admitted. She said something so softly that Ben couldn't understand, but that he assumed was a brief prayer. Carolyn crossed herself. Belief in God was real to her, uncompromised in all ways but one. Though knowing Ben professed to believe in Christianity, she knew Ben was very uncomfortable discussing her strong faith and her willingness to express it. He knew that influenced her to practice its enjoyment in silence in his presence. Ben wondered if she ever considered why this made him so uncomfortable.

Ben and Carolyn watched the Indian trudge across the field until he disappeared into the woods line. They went back to their camping activities with less enthusiasm. The man hadn't been hostile or even unpleasant. His warning threats were heavily veiled, but he left Carolyn and Ben with the feeling that his presence was sinister. Neither looked forward to encountering him again; both felt that they would. Dread of the seemingly inoffensive figure had infiltrated their psyche.

# # # # #

Chapter   10

The First Night

Ben sat slumped in his camp chair, his hand holding an aluminum cup full of bourbon and water. He stared into the campfire. Restless discontent and depression clung to him for no reason to which he would consciously admit. Alcohol intensified that effect on Ben; it also made him more combative. With nothing to distract him or hold his interest, he stewed in his melancholy mood.

The two youngest children had bedded down in the kids' tent two hours earlier. Angela left the fire and joined her siblings in their quarters an hour later. She played the hard-rock and hip-hop music she liked, the squalling noise filtering out to the fireside. He marveled that the beat and bluster didn't wake Danny or Melanie. Ben hated his daughter's taste in music, but couldn't find a rational reason to deny her the right to listen. Finally, her radio had gone silent. Ben said, "Hooray, I'd had about enough of the shit that passes for rock now days." He wouldn't have to yell at her. In a way he felt denied the privilege.

The clink and clank of metal on metal annoyed Ben as Carolyn stored the pots and pans she finished cleaning. The bourbon he drank made him surly, irritable, and thinned his patience. Ben made a face at Carolyn and shook his head. After a few more pings and bangs he said, "Christ, Carolyn, can't you make more racket?"

"Sorry," She said.

"Are you about done?" "Uh-huh."

Ben was on edge and he gradually, grudgingly acknowledged why. When he'd begun to relax and sip his drink, he had no focus for his mind. It searched for something to dwell on. It grasped the one unresolved event of the day; their visit from the Seminole. The Indian's words regarding evil and their campsite being "a place no one should go," were getting to him, though he knew he shouldn't allow that to happen. He figured a few more drinks would relax him, wash his concerns away; so far they hadn't worked. Ben downed the contents of his cup, reached for the bottle of Jack Daniels and picked up the full milk jug of water resting by his feet. The buzz running through his body made balancing the cup on his knees a chore. He poured whiskey on his pants as well as in the aluminum. Ben splashed water on top, spilling a third of the mixture on his legs. He growled, "Ahhhh, Shit!" Ben sipped from the cup and stared at the flames. The dreaded unknown wouldn't leave: he heard the Seminole's words and saw his copper-skinned face. "Shit," he muttered again.

"Do you want your radio?" Carolyn asked.

"Yeah." Ben belched. A mixture of fish fillets, hush puppies, French fries, green beans, and bourbon rolled around in his stomach. While he waited for Carolyn's return, he thought about what he'd like to listen. No news or talk. Politics, the economy, international events, and other disasters were too depressing. He decided he'd enjoy some of his kind of music. Ben rubbed his boot toe in the sand, becoming increasingly impatient. What was Carolyn doing after she'd made her offer?

Oldies. That was what he wanted. After idling time away by looking at the sand patterns his hikers made, he grumbled, "When the hell are you coming, next year?"

She was standing next to him. Ben hadn't heard Carolyn's approach or knew she was patiently waiting when he made his smartassed remark.

"Here you go," she said and extended the radio toward him, frowning at Ben as she spoke.

His body jerked at the sound of her voice. "Oh, I didn't know you were here." Ben twisted around, took the radio from her, and nodded. "Thanks," he mumbled. Ben felt like an ass, knowing he was out-of-line. His wife was a good one, one that he knew he should treat better than he did. The word sorry froze on his lips, however.

Carolyn stood statue-like, the firelight dancing on her face, her hair, and body. Backlit from the gas lantern hung in the oak limbs behind her, as well as the campfire, he thought, she sure hasn't lost her looks. A lot of his friends' wives quit trying after a few years of marriage. They got fat, sloppy, and let themselves go, seeming to have lost pride and interest in their appearance. Not Carolyn. She still had a great figure, kept her hair just so, and dressed snappily. Ben was glad she was his.

Ben pushed the power button and the radio crackled. He twisted the dial to his favorite oldies station. The music was there, but the reception was faint and so marred with static, listening wasn't practical. Ben looked at the sky. It was moonless—pitch dark, but full of stars. There weren't any clouds to hamper reception, not that he was sure they would hurt the signal anyway. He'd gotten fine reception on the same frequency that afternoon. Ben tried several other stations with the same result. It had to be something in the atmosphere, he decided. Local call letters had been on the air that afternoon, but after a couple of twisting journeys up and down the dial, he grunted in disgust. "Shit! These yokel stations must stop broadcasting at night," he grumbled. Ben sighed, turned the radio off, and gave up, dropping it to the ground in disgust.

"What time are we getting up tomorrow?" Carolyn asked.

"No reason to get up early." Ben kicked the radio next to his chair. "Whenever we wake up."

"Good." Carolyn stretched her arms back over her head and yawned. "I'm going to go to bed. I'm tired." She looked at him and added, "Don't stay out here too long. I'd like you to come in the tent with me. This spot...well...I'm still a little scared."

"There's nothing out here but us." Ben reached over and grabbed her jeans crotch. "I'll be in before long."

Carolyn frowned and twisted away. "I've told you I wish you wouldn't do that."

"Hell, Carolyn, there's no one around." Ben leered at her. "Just get it ready for me." He raised his eyebrows and smiled suggestively. "If you want another Melanie or Danny, fine. My birth control is back at the house." She walked toward the tent, turning off the lantern as she went. "Please don't stay up too late," Carolyn said as she unzipped the door screen and disappeared inside the cloth cave.

# # # # #

Chapter 11

Ben laughed to himself and took another sip of bourbon. Thinking about the sex he'd have with Carolyn later relaxed him. She'd moan and complain, but he knew what buttons to push to secure her compliance. It never occurred to him that she hadn't initiated intimacy between them in years. It was all about conquest, anyways, and if she took on the role of initiator then his own role was diminished. Their sexual routine worked well for him. He never asked if it worked as well for his wife. The thought of an experience of sharing rather than overcoming never entered his mind.

He extended a boot and shoved a partially burnt log deeper into the fire. An explosion of sparks flew off in the rising waves of heat. A big roaring campfire provided some of Ben's favorite outdoor moments. Ben and his slave labor had gathered plenty of firewood that afternoon and he could burn as much as he pleased. He figured he wouldn't use a third of the wood available.

A mystic power existed in campfire flames. Ben believed man's hypnotic fascination with fire was passed down through human generations in their DNA. He envisioned early man crouched around their fire in a cave or on a plain. It was the center of their lives providing warmth and protection in a cold and dangerous world. The fire gave them comfort and pleasure and it did the same for him. It helped him not to think. It helped him forget the Indian and his nagging apprehension regarding the campsite.

His mind wandered to work and some problems that needed attention. The new salesman who replaced Bill Miller was beginning to be more than an aggravation. Ben disliked the man the moment he met him. From what Ben could tell the feeling was mutual. The man was older and the two didn't share the same interests or values. Ben's boss realigned the customer accounts after Miller died, giving Ben some of Miller's best accounts and taking away some of Ben's least productive ones. The new man got the leftovers and discards, plus a small territory no one had tried to sell in before. Frank, the new man, got the shaft to Ben's way of thinking.

Much to Ben's chagrin, Frank did better than "well" with his new territory, plus Bill Miller's and Ben's castoff accounts. Within a month, Frank's volume approached Ben's and the fact that some of the biggest contributors to Frank's achievement were Ben's discards made it more infuriating. Ben had spent years cultivating some of them without success. Frank was rapidly becoming the boss's new champion. It burned Ben... particularly in light of the small company's recent fast growth rate. The boss had been speaking to Ben about the need for adding a Sales Manager in the future. All these conversations stopped abruptly. Frank was a threat—and he had to deal with it.

Ben saw the need to take the luster off Frank's performance. He sat staring into the fire thinking about additional ways to bring this about. Seeds had already been planted. Frank had a few problems with the delivery department supervisor. The new salesman pressured the woman to schedule his sales first and to give his customers added perks, like moving the loads off the receiving docks for them. The lady, Sandra, didn't push easily or gracefully. Ben stoked this smoldering conflict with a few half-truths whispered in the woman's ear. Some less than complimentary voicemail comments Frank made about her appearance, uttered into Ben's answering machine in a moment of frustration, were too good of a weapon to not be used. Ben would replay them for her clandestinely and bring the situation to a boil.

Ben also started dissension between Frank and a purchasing agent who worked with one of Ben's ex-customers. The purchasing agent for this company, the largest contributor to Frank's sales volume, was gay. That was not a widely known fact, nor did the buyer want it to be. No embarrassment was involved, for the man was proud to be gay; he simply wanted his private life to remain private. Ben called the man and let it "slip" that he thought Frank hated gays. He grinned as he recalled the phone conversation.

"How you doing with Frank?" Ben asked in the most innocent sounding voice he could.

"Fine," the buyer said cheerily. "Frank seems to be a good guy and a hard worker."

"That's good. I was concerned there might be a problem," Ben cast out the bait.

"Oh…Why's that?"

"No reason. Just, if anything goes wrong let me know and I'll try to fix it." Ben knew he had the man hooked.

"What's up?" the man asked suspiciously.

"Aaaahhhh." Ben took a deep breath as though he was having a difficult time disclosing what he had to say when the fact was he had difficulty restraining himself from belching out his story. "I don't like to…well…Frank doesn't care for homosexuals. I mean he really doesn't."

There was complete quiet on the other end of the line. Ben honed his lie. "Frank's from an older generation than us. He doesn't understand people that don't think like him. That's strictly from comments he's made. Or, at least, that's what I got from what he said. I could be wrong, but… I never said anything regarding you, because I know your thoughts about keeping your life, your life. But…just-in-case, call me if there's…an issue."

None of what Ben said was true, but the damage would be done even if the truth surfaced at some later date. His carefully worded comments gave him deniability. Concurrently, Ben encouraged Frank to tell the man gay jokes and make disparaging remarks about homosexuals. Frank had nodded and said he wasn't into making fun of people, but he'd consider making a joke or two. Ben figured it wouldn't take long for Frank to lose his largest account. Yep… He would see that Frank got his. Ben had a twinge of conscience; the purchasing agent was a nice guy, but—that was just one of those things. Ben sipped more bourbon. All was fair in love, war, and business.

The only thing good about Frank was his new sales assistant. She was in her early twenties, attractive enough, and a possessor of what Bill Miller always referred to as a "million dollar ass." Her name, August, was as hot and sultry as he envisioned she'd be when he finally got her in the sack. She'd be a project, but worth the effort. Ben visualized her naked body and the things he'd do with her. His body reacted. Maybe it was time to go to bed. He took another sip of bourbon.

Ben looked up through the canopy of oak branches at the dark sky. It was a beautiful night for camping. The Florida February air was cool, but not uncomfortable—it would make for great sleeping when he finally curled up inside his bag. He looked out over the prairie toward the oak and cypress forest. Low on the horizon, two points of white light caught his eye. At first he thought the lights were an airplane landing at the small regional airport, but decided the strip was located too far away to be able to see activity there. Maybe the lights came from a plane landing on a private strip. He watched them until they dipped behind the tree line.

He looked down at his cup to take a sip of bourbon. As he did so, Ben heard something. He strained his ears. It sounded like many voices, talking, crying, even screaming, but so low it was almost inaudible. Ben decided to check the radio. Maybe he'd left the power on and the atmospheric conditions had cleared enough to listen. He picked the black plastic box up, but found the switch was turned to 'off.' Ben held the speaker up to his ear. The noise was coming from the radio. He could hear the very faint jumble of voices speaking in foreign languages. That was not unusual in Southwest Florida. There were nearly as many Spanish language stations as those broadcasting in English. However, Ben understood a little Spanish and it didn't sound like that language. Not exclusively. He strained his ears, but the sound remained so faint he couldn't make out any words in the continuous buzz. How was that possible, the switch was turned off? He turned the power on and off to be sure. The noise continued at a barely audible level regardless of the button's position. The radio must be broken. Ben examined the exterior, dials, switches, and antennae, but couldn't see anything wrong in the firelight. He decided he needed the flashlight.

When Ben stood up to get the light from the camp table, he spilled the contents of his cup on his thigh and noticed his legs were very unstable. He watched the cup tumble in slow motion until it hit the sand next to the fire. The world wanted to rotate and rock. Old Jack Daniels was catching up with him. "I'm drunk," Ben said to the night air. He made the twenty unsteady steps required to get the flashlight and return to his camp chair. Ben picked the radio up again, examining it in the flashlight's beam. He turned the dial. The same noise came from the radio no matter where he tuned it. The damn thing was broke, but how? Ben bent over to lay it back down, saying, "Piece of shit," and dropped it the last few inches. At least they still had Angela's radio to use for the rest of the trip.

Ben looked above the tree line where the lights had been previously. They were gone; no others took their place. Only pin-pricks of star light were twinkling above the tree line. He idly scanned the prairie from left to right. Ben's eyes jolted to a stop about two thirds of the way around. Two small luminous objects were suspended off the ground, side by side, and appeared to be advancing toward the campsite. Glowing shades of purple, violet, and crimson pulsed from what appeared to emanate from burning dots in the white light's center. He blinked several times to be sure he was seeing something. What he watched was too high off the ground and too close together to be a vehicle. The glow coming from the circles certainly didn't look like it came from headlights.

As far as he could determine, the globes advanced steadily and smoothly toward the camp, though he had no idea how far away they were.

While distinctly illuminated, no beam of light shone out of them, like a flashlight would create. Ben strained his eyes trying to determine what was coming toward him. Whatever the object was, it floated over the prairie without any bounce or sway. No noise accompanied the specter's movement. It moved too fast to be carried by a person walking. As it approached, he saw another detail, spots of darkness in the centers of each light, but the distance was too great to see exactly what they were. Ben stood up, took a couple of steps forward, squinted, and blinked. He still couldn't identify the objects—or even if they were real. He'd heard of something called St. Elmo's fire. The only thing he knew for sure was that the lights were steadily moving closer.

It must be the damned Indian, Ben decided. Maybe the bastard had some friends helping him. The Indian told them he was some kind of an engineer. He'd probably rigged up some type of an elaborate hoax. It was obvious he wanted them to leave. Ben's mind raced. Why was it so important to the Indian that they move from this particular campsite? And why go to such an effort to scare them? The Indian could have simply told them they were trespassing, to pack up, and get out. There wouldn't have been an alternative; his family would have had to leave. It didn't make sense.

Maybe, Ben thought, I'm imagining the whole thing. Maybe a combination of the bourbon and the apprehension the Indian planted were bending his mind. He never experienced a hallucination from bourbon or any other alcohol, but Ben had been through a bout with the unreal. When he was young, very young, a combination of drugs and trying them in a graveyard provided an experience so frightening he never experimented with substances again. The monsters, ghouls, and ghosts he'd seen in movies and on TV suddenly came alive, appearing all around him, stepping out of graves, chasing him, terrifying him. In a panic, he crashed into a tombstone. The result was a huge scar he still carried on his scalp. It took three friends to subdue and immobilize him for a couple of hours or he might have done more serious damage to himself.

The lights still moved toward him, but at a slower pace. It was the damned Indian. He was sure of it. Ben shook his fist in the lights' direction. "Fuck you," he shouted. He turned his back on them and stepped back to his chair. The children's tent was quiet and Carolyn's gentle snore told him he was the only one tortured by whatever stalked the camp. Should he wake Carolyn? Nothing would come of it, why scare her? She would want to leave immediately. Ben set his jaw. The red son-of-a-bitch wasn't going to drive him away. Period. Should he get his gun? Ben spun around to confront the lights. One of his bourbon encumbered feet found the edge of the campfire and he did an awkward little dance to remove his heated boot.

When he looked up, the lights had disappeared. He snorted disgustedly and flopped back into the camp chair. It didn't take much to discourage the bastard, Ben decided. He tried to visualize the Seminole skulking away, angry and disappointed that his ruse was unsuccessful. "It was the fucking Indian," he grunted to the deaf campfire. Ben refilled his cup with Jack Daniels and tossed a couple more logs on the fire. He decided the first lights he saw were different, probably airplanes. The ones on the prairie, those were the Indian, those were designed to scare him away.

#

Chapter   12

Sitting by the fire a few more minutes would assure the red asshole didn't return. Even though Ben felt relatively sure the Indian, or those who might be with him, wouldn't hurt him and his family, he still felt uneasy. What would they do? Try to scare them again? Spy on the camp? He sat staring into the fire, watching the various shades of yellows, oranges, blues, and reds rise and fall, flickering up from the wood. Occasionally, he would look out to where he last saw the lights. Nothing was there. Whatever. Nothing was visible.

Time passed without the phantom lights' reappearance. Maybe it stalked them in the darkness would have to cross the creek to get into the campsite. Ben was sure he'd hear the splashing if it attempted to wade or swim the stream. He methodically checked on either side of where the glowing spots disappeared. Was it swamp gas. Was it called St. Elmo's fire? He tried to remember if that was correct for the phenomenon's name. It was St.

Somebody's Fire. Anne's? Edgar's? No, it was Elmo's. He seemed to remember that it had something to do with lightning, but he couldn't recall the specifics. He was tired and addled; Ben's head nodded. Bourbon and the day's exertions, physical and mental, dulled his mind and weighted his eyelids. His chin dipped until it touched his chest. The contact jarred him awake with a startled awareness, not realizing what had interrupted his stupor.

Instinctively, Ben shook his head to clear sleep away. He sat there for several seconds, slumber trying to pull him back into blackness, before his conscious thought told him it was time for the tent and his sleeping bag. The Seminole had evidently abandoned his efforts to intimidate him and his family. It was safe to get some rest. Ben struggled out of his chair, clutching his flashlight, and watching his feet so he wouldn't step in the fire again. He followed the flashlight beam along the ground to the tent. Carolyn's continued snoring floated through the fabric walls assuring him all was well. Ben hunkered down to unzip the closed tent entrance. He turned the flashlight off so it wouldn't disturb Carolyn. Ben's liquor clumsy hands fumbled with the tent door. Fabric caught in the zipper as he tugged and pulled. He dropped the flashlight to have both hands available to free the mechanism.

Ben straightened back up as he pulled the zipper to the opening's top. Blood drained from his head for a second and this added to his dizziness. He shook his head vigorously to clear it. Before going inside, Ben looked behind the tent toward the fields beyond. What he saw sobered him, cleared his vision, and sent blood pounding to his brain.

The two luminous globes gleamed from directly behind the campsite, only thirty feet away.   There was no doubt about what they were at that distance. The light emanated from the eyes of some creature… a huge creature. The eyes were larger than softballs and were elevated eight feet off the ground. Irises that flashed different hues of crimson, violet, and maroon surrounded dark pupils, shiny and black. Tiny red lines wound through the luminous whites like spider web. Separated by a foot wide space, they were fierce, angry, and humanoid. Except for the color change in the irises, Ben couldn't detect any movement. He took a slow, shocked step backwards. "Oh, shit," he murmured, "Shit, shit, shit." The eyes were threatening, malevolent, and savage. Worst of all, the pupils locked themselves on Ben's eyes in unrelenting contact. Frozen with fear and indecision, Ben could not look away from them. His feet rooted to the ground.

Though the presence before him looked as though it wished to do him harm, it did not advance. Ben blinked. The apparition didn't go away. Ben strained his eyes to see the outline of what stood before him, but he could discern nothing. No shape, no boundary, no outline. Inky black darkness swallowed the view of what lay behind the fierce eyes. It watched him, and he it. Seconds were hours to Ben. He waited, helplessly, for the thing to come at him, to attack him, to tear him to shreds, to devour him. It did nothing but glare at Ben with immeasurable hate. He wondered if the thing would chase him or if it would stay to attack those sleeping in the tents if he tried to flee.

It struck Ben—the children and his wife were asleep. This thing, this presence made no sound to wake them. Nothing. There was no noise, not even the ever-present nighttime drone of insects always heard on camping trips. The silence was like that of the grave.

Ben watched the entity for any movement. None came. They stared at each other, one in mortal fear, the other exuding mindless, vicious aggression. Time passed. Ben became frantic to see what threatened him. The flashlight lay at his feet. He knew he had to pick it up and let its beam disclose what manner of creature faced him no matter how ominous it might be. In order to grab the light, he'd temporarily lose sight of the malevolent thing; Ben wondered if the eye contact he was maintaining kept it from advancing and attacking. Ben held steady, hoping it would go away, but knowing it would not. At last, he made the decision. He would slowly move down toward the light until he lost sight of the eyes, drop quickly, then immediately spring up with the light on, illuminating what threatened him. His knees flexed. The specter's pupils followed his movement, but the eyes remained static. When he reached the limit of his ability to maintain eye contact with the thing, he dropped to the ground, his hands grasping for the flashlight. No noise or sign of attack came as he pushed the switch forward and leaped upward.

The eyes were gone. He pointed the flashlight at where they had been. Nothing was there, not even the beam of light. Ben mashed the on-off button and turned the light into his face to see what was wrong. The light glared in his eyes blinding him for a split second and in one motion he swung the light back at the location. This time it disclosed what he would have expected to see anytime. Sand, weeds in the fields beyond, the trunk of one of the great oaks, but nothing else. He shook his head, trying to clear the bourbon from his brain and sharpen his thought process. Maybe he hadn't turned the light switch on the first time. Where had the specter gone? Behind me! Ben whirled around. The light beam disclosed the camp and its expected surroundings, nothing else. He whipped back around expecting to see the eyes reappear at the spot he last saw them. They were gone. He jerked the light to either side. Nothing. Ben quickly circled the camp's perimeter with the flash light's beam, his intense stare following its movement. He repeated the sweep at a slower speed, and then meticulously shined the light around the campsite a final time, hesitating at every potential point of concealment. There was nothing.

Ben stood, afraid to move and afraid not to. The realization that the liquor's influence was lessening significantly dawned on him. Maybe the whole thing was a hallucination. An alcohol induced fantasy. He had to find out.

Ben took a few halting, hesitant steps toward where the specter had been. Nothing. He jerked around, half expecting the eyes to be glaring from some other vantage point. Nothing. Slowly, Ben walked to the spot where he saw the vision. If something so huge had been there, tracks and signs of its presence were sure to be in evidence in the soft powder-like sand that covered the mound. Nothing. The flashlight beam probed the surrounding area, racing from point to point. Nothing. Ben walked the whole circumference of the camp, carefully examining the ground and the camp's margins. Nothing.

He cut back through the camp, passing the fire, the chair, and the bourbon bottle. Ben took an angry swipe at the bottle with his foot…but missed. He wouldn't make the mistake of getting drunk tomorrow night. It was a hallucination. It had to be. Ben hesitated a second before entering the tent. He took a final look at the area where he'd last seen the eyes. Nothing. He shook his head in disgust and entered the tent, ninety-five percent sure what he saw, the menacing image, was only in his mind. But that other five percent remained.

# # # # #

Chapter 13

Adrenalin and uncertainty kept him awake after he slid into his sleeping bag. Any thoughts of sex with Carolyn were forgotten. When sleep came it was fitful and disturbed. Dreams, old and new, haunted his slumber. His parents appeared and admonished him for failing to live to their diametrically opposed tenants. Ben's mother implored him to change his behavior and to pray for salvation. His father sneered and made fun of her protestations of faith. They turned to skeletons chasing him through his nightmare. Ghouls appeared, joining the race as he desperately tried to escape. He woke, fell back to sleep, hoping that the visions would go away, but they returned and then were replaced by the new nemesis lurking in the prairie darkness. This threat jolted him awake again.

"Are you okay?" Carolyn asked.

"Yes," Ben answered. He heard Carolyn move in her sleeping bag.

"You're talking and yelling in your sleep." She sounded sleepy. "Bad dreams?"

"Uh-huh," Ben said. He forced his eyes open, trying not to revisit the land of terror sleep took him to. His struggle to maintain consciousness came in spurts as his lids became heavier and his fear of revisiting the specters in his dreams gripped him. Each effort came with lessening resolve.

He considered praying, but the thought he'd rely on that as a "way out" of his problem, when he had his doubts, forced him to reject succumbing to his desire. He asked the silent question, would God look at him as a hypocrite based on his behavior? It didn't occur to him to change his behavior permanently or what purpose faith offered. Ben couldn't resolve his problem so the prayer went unsaid.

Eventually, exhaustion caught him with its full force and provided rest in the last vestiges of night. His closed eyes and his demons agreed to a truce.

# # # # #

Chapter   14

At The Place, The Second Day

In the morning, Ben had rested, but was not refreshed. This kept him in his cot long after his normal first-light-of-day rising. He pulled his sleeping bag over his head, catching moments of slumber interrupted by camp noises. When he finally swung his legs out of his cot, his family was up and dressed, even the sleepy-headed Angela. Carolyn had the bacon fried and was preparing scrambled eggs as he emerged from the tent.

"I was just getting ready to check on you," Carolyn said as he walked up. She reached up and kissed him on the cheek, handed him a cup of coffee, said "It's a great morning, dear," and returned to her cooking. Humming a song, bustling around the stove, and making occasional visits to the rejuvenated campfire to warm her hands, Carolyn looked completely relaxed. The two youngest children romped around, involved in some carefree game that utilized their fertile imaginations. Angela sat catatonically, slumped in a camp chair, absorbing heat from the fire. Ben realized he was the only one made uneasy by their surroundings.

Ben took a sip of coffee and asked Carolyn, "You sleep good last night?"

"I slept like a log."

"No strange noises or anything unusual happened to bother you?"

"Nothing. Well, your mumblings woke me a couple times, but I went right back to sleep. All my fretting about this spot was foolish, wasn't it?"

Ben nodded, but remained silent. His story would have a negative effect on his family's sense of security. He didn't want that. Last night's events were almost certainly produced by bourbon and his imagination. If he confessed to having such a wild delusion it would rupture his pride That sealed his lips even tighter. Ben's queasy stomach and dull headache, the bourbon's last punishing effects, underlined the probability his experience was a mental hob-goblin, not the work of the Indian or a spirit roaming the campsite.

"Breakfast's ready," Carolyn announced as she carried the last two plates to the table.

The family assembled around its white plastic top and sat down in front of eggs, bacon, and grits.

Angela removed the paper towel covering her plate to keep her breakfast warm. She turned her nose up and frowned. "You know I could be at Betty's this morning. Her mother always has eggs Benedict and strawberry pancakes the morning after a sleep over."

Carolyn glanced at her husband, expecting him to rebuke Angela and lecture her on the virtue of the family outings they went on, but Ben stared in space, disconnected from the world around him. She looked at him and blinked, but said nothing.

"Where are we going to fish today, Dad?" Danny asked. Ben didn't hear him or the boy's words didn't register.

"Hey, Dad." Danny cocked his head sideways and looked at his father questioningly.

"Honey, are you alright?" Carolyn got no more response than her son. She reached over the table, poked his forearm with her finger, and repeated, "Honey, are you alright?"

"Shit, what?" he snapped returning from whatever universe he'd traveled to.

"Danny asked where you're going to fish today."

"I don't know. I'll figure it out later," Ben said, frowning as he took his first look at his breakfast.

"Ben. Are you feeling okay?" Carolyn asked again, her face showing concern.

"No! I drank too much fu…I drank too much damn bourbon last night. I've got a bad hangover. I'd appreciate it if you'd just leave me alone for a while."

"Okay, we can do that," Carolyn agreed. She looked at the children and said, "You heard your father. He's having a bad hair day. Let's let him recuperate for a bit."

Angela rolled her eyes and snorted. Carolyn cautioned, "None of that, young lady."

Melanie asked, "Do I have to eat all my egg?" and things went back to 'normal' for the rest of the family.

Ben brooded through breakfast, remaining uncharacteristically quiet. It was apparent Ben was troubled and distracted, but, to some degree, his wife and kids welcomed release from his domineering behavior that normally accompanied family activities. It was a bit unsettling for Carolyn who couldn't help wondering if an explosion would follow.

When preparing for the day's fishing, Ben walked around the canoes like a robot, lacking the zeal he normally exhibited. His wife and children watched him not quite knowing what to think of the "stranger" who they were camping with.

Carolyn couldn't let his unusual behavior go unchallenged. As Ben and Carolyn pushed away from shore, she said. "You're awfully quiet this morning. I've seen you hung over many times, but never like this. Something else is bothering you, isn't it?"

"No."

"You sure? You don't seem to be yourself."

"Shit, Carolyn, can't I just relax sometime." Ben snarled and frowned.

"Sure." Carolyn decided her attempt to help wasn't worth the effort. She decided she'd enjoy the lack of his constant commands and Ben's not interfering with every action taken by her and the children. Besides, his surly behavior meant he hadn't strayed too far from normal.

# # # # #

Chapter   15

The day proved to be a very pleasant, warm one. The Callisons shed their windbreakers and sweaters long before noon. A gentle breeze kept them in long sleeves, but not chilled or uncomfortable. With the exception of Ben's behavior, the day went as any other camping trip would. His reclusive and depressed mood lessened as the day progressed, for the outdoors was extra friendly and nature provided bountiful entertainment on the isolated little prairie. Fishing remained excellent. It was so good there wasn't need to take the canoes far from their campsite, though the fish continued to avoid waters adjacent to the mound their tents were pitched on.

The family spotted several deer and a flock of turkey at various times during the day. Ospreys, red tailed hawks, and even a bald eagle flew overhead while 'gators, turtles, and the rest of the creek and swamp creatures crawled, ran, and swam in profuse numbers. Carolyn and the children thoroughly enjoyed the day…Ben a little less.

Nagging doubt persisted, damping his spirits. Though Ben told himself everything he experienced was an alcohol-dampened dream and he would avoid any replay by staying completely sober that evening, his uneasiness grew as the afternoon passed. He tried to dismiss his fears and erase the memory of the previous night, but the sheer terror he experienced wouldn't allow it. Each tick of the clock added an additional grain of sand to the growing dull weight of apprehension.

He thought of breaking camp, of leaving. Though he wanted to, his machismo prevented him from making the suggestion. He was trapped by his words and braggadocio, a situation he found himself in all too frequently. Ben knew he would be forced to endure his fears without family support—they couldn't help if they weren't aware and he wasn't willing to inform them—and this deepened his problem.

The complete lack of other human presence on the little prairie would have normally been welcomed by Ben. Not so this day. The Callisons were The Swiss Family Robinson in the little world surrounded by woods and swamps bordering the prairie. Not a single soul appeared. Usually a boat-load of fisherman would wander by the family's normal campsite, but the additional distance and the No

Trespassing sign probably kept others from venturing to where they were camped. The only evidence of the human world outside was a light plane seen at a long distance.

Ben expected the Indian to return. Though he believed alcohol created his hallucination, the possibility remained that his terror-filled night could have been created by that man's cruel prank. If so, the Seminole would return to see if his attempts to dislodge them from the site were successful. Ben wanted the man to be bitterly disappointed, though the thought that the Indian perpetrated what he saw the previous evening posed the possibility of a replay, or worse, could be in-store for the coming night. A third, very slim possibility was that some unexplainable super-natural event had occurred. That was horrifying. Shuddering, Ben didn't want to accept that or think about it further.

"You're shaking. Are you getting sick?" Carolyn stood in front of Ben who was sitting in the oak tree's shade.

"No!" Ben snapped. He readjusted his attitude. "It's cooler in the shade than I thought. I'm going to move into the sun."

Carolyn said nothing but peered at him skeptically.

"Okay, I've been thinking about some things going on at work. Some problems. Nothing huge, but something I need to handle." Ben watched Carolyn's face. The lie satisfied her. She went about her camping activities; he proceeded to boil mentally creating tension within. His stress was increasing to a crescendo with each passing hour.

Ben watched for the Indian more frequently as the day progressed, but unless the man remained at a great distance, spying on them from the woods, the Seminole had evidently lost interest. Ben told himself the man's failure to reappear proved the previous night's visions were hallucinations, something he could avoid by leaving the bourbon in the bottle. Things would be fine this coming night. But Ben remembered the Indian's answer about dangers in the place they were camped, "No lady, only after dark."

As evening approached, Ben's fear became fevered. Panic, though he refused to admit it, lived in him. He reexamined the possibility of leaving. What excuse could he use? He'd been bragging about how "caught up" he was at home, eliminating that as a possible reason. His past reaction to his family being sick or uncomfortable on a camping trip robbed him of that possibility. Ben's favorite response to the sufferer was, "Suck it up, sissy." Ben knew he'd get the same unsympathetic reaction to any attempt to return home for those causes. He searched for another reason to leave without divulging his fears or rupturing his sense of masculinity. In the end, Ben couldn't face the thought of reducing the iron-man image he believed his family held of him by mentioning his desire to leave.

He told himself doubts that he'd experienced anything but a hallucination were stupid. Replaying the scenario over and over as he had all day wouldn't help. He did his best to believe this. Ben wasn't successful, for as the sun fell on the horizon, his uneasiness rose and the last of his peace of mind departed.

# # # # #

Chapter   16

"I'm going to go sit by the creek." Ben carried
his camp chair to the western edge of the campsite
where he could watch the sunset. He was desperate to
find solace. Carolyn was busy cleaning supper's pots
and pans and chatting with Danny and Melanie.
Angela already retreated to the children's tent to
listen to what she considered good music and to read
a book. Watching the sun and the day's end myriad
of colors normally cleansed and relaxed Ben, but he
was alone with his thoughts and they would give him
no peace. They played over and over in his mind like
an old-fashioned record player stuck on the same
passage of a song.

"Beautiful. It is a beautiful damned place. God
and nature make things that can't be duplicated." Ben
spoke to himself hoping the sound of his own words
might bring relief. What he saw was sunlight that
glittered on the narrow creek as the last rays bounced
across its waters. The fireball above the tree line,
increased in size by the atmosphere's curvature optic

effect, turned the clouds brilliant and spectacular colors. Vibrant but delicate pinks, salmons, blues and violets painted the sky in a way no man could emulate. It was an act of God and this disturbed Ben. God was the reason for his concern for the coming night... if bourbon hadn't spawned his previous night's terror.

That concern was rooted in the Indian's words: Only the purest of heart, those with no evil in them, are free to come here. It shouldn't have bothered him. If his sense of logic had truly convinced his mind that the previous traumatic night was a hallucination that flowed from the bourbon bottle, he wouldn't have worried that a replay would happen. But some thoughts are like a splinter lodged in the mind, any exercise reminds the sufferer of its presence and its difficulty to remove.

The concept of God's good and the Devil's evil pricked Ben's mind. He didn't consider himself evil by man's standards. He didn't break man's laws. The worst he did was drive under the influence occasionally and drive over the speed limit. Everyone did these things. Surely this didn't make him evil. His actions at work were simply business. People constantly jockeyed for position in that cutthroat world. It was part of advancing your employment position. Ben knew that many others did the same things to get ahead. By business standards, he concluded, he didn't engage in evilness.

The affairs he indulged in were harmless trysts. He never approached a woman who didn't send clear signals she would welcome an advance. That didn't mean he wouldn't court her interest. Ben stayed away from married women most of the time so there wouldn't be complications. He never gave a woman false hope regarding the relationship. Sex was what it was about and he made this clear. He loved Carolyn and wouldn't consider leaving her. The little trips outside the fence made him a better lover, Ben believed. It was better for Carolyn and their marriage. The only girl he ever took advantage of was a high school classmate twenty years ago. She'd taken her clothes off voluntarily and was all for it until the last second. Ben simply didn't let her change her mind. Any man and most women understood that. It didn't make him evil... not in man's eyes. In fact, his father believed that this behavior proved an individual's manhood. But, what about God's view?

As the sun settled behind the tree line and the sky repainted its self countless times in innumerable hues, the whole concept of God, God's reality, and God's laws, thrust itself into his consciousness. Was the panorama Ben saw before him an omen thrust into his mind by an omnipotent force making the question of religious evil impossible to ignore? He knew he must answer it.

What was acceptable in man's secular view wasn't acceptable when examined under the microscope of religion. Judeo-Christianity's Ten Commandments placed the mantel of evil squarely around his shoulders. He clearly violated four of those rules regularly. The unsettling thing was how universal these beliefs were. Islam, Hindu, Buddhism, almost all religions had such doctrine. If a God existed, Ben was evil by His rules.

"Are you up there?" Ben spoke to the sky which changed its colors and answer with every micro degree the sun fell behind the horizon. Did God exist? If he did, what type of an entity was this all powerful force? Ben had more questions than answers about God's existence. The concept of an omnipotent being watching all humanity constantly went beyond Ben's belief. If such a being existed and if God passed down the laws man lived by, how could God allow evil things to happen? Even if he passed over small everyday transgressions based on the concept of free will, how could such a being allow a Hitler or a Stalin to perpetrate such huge evils? How could the rule-making God, a loving God, not take action to stop such things?

But when Ben looked at the design of the human body, of the intricacies and delicate balance of nature, it was impossible for him to deny the probability of intelligent design. Things just didn't "happen" to fall together in a random way. Those two major pieces of evidence clashed in his mind and he couldn't reconcile them. Though he resisted making a decision, the happenings of the previous day and night created urgency within him to reaffirm his choice of a code; man's or God's.

His mother's teachings and her insistence that he be educated as a staunch Catholic were strong traces pulling against the halter that was his chosen moral compass. He knew right from wrong in religious terms, but he'd made his choice twenty years ago. That choice was to pattern his mores after his father. After his bending of God's rules as a high school junior and enjoying the "benefits" derived from cheating, lying, manipulating, and promiscuity, he saw his path clearly. His mother's youthful religious teachings were dismissible, but still bred nagging, uncomfortable guilt in his soul. Carolyn's belief in salvation through Christ was a mirror of his mother's faith that he was forced to stare at constantly, maintaining his underlying discomfort at the life-style he'd chosen.

One thing he couldn't deny was the dependence of man's law on God's law. Most criminal statutes had root in religious concepts. If one accepted that as true, the evil that God recognized and the evil man recognized were the same. And, if that were true, his explanations to his conscience were hollow lies to justify his pleasures rather than honest statements of modern necessity and reality.   If that were true...

Carolyn's touch on his shoulder interrupted Ben's contemplations and provided a welcome relief from the struggle raging in his conscience. She carried a chair in her other hand and smiled down at him as she stood by his side. "Mind?" she asked. "No." Ben smiled and shook his head.

Carolyn placed her chair next to him. "Beautiful," she said as she settled in her seat, her eyes on the horizon. "The Lord is painting a particularly pretty picture tonight."
Ben looked at her for several seconds before asking, "Do you really believe there's someone up there, operating everything, watching everything."

"Don't you? Look at that."

"That could be just a pure random happening."

"I guess it could. If you think of God as an engineer running a train, controlling the scream of every whistle and the toll of every bell...I don't think of him that way. He made everything then he lets it work."

Including us?"

"Most importantly us." Carolyn took her eyes off the sky to wink at him.
"What if there isn't a God? What if you find out its all story?

Wouldn't you feel cheated in some way?"

"No, Ben. I've thought about the possibility, I won't deny that. But, do I lose if I believe in God? I don't think so. It helps me live my life in a manner I'm comfortable with and is acceptable to most of my fellow man. Having hope and faith in God give me strength. I like that. I chose to believe. If I die and there isn't a heaven, I haven't lost a thing, have I?"

Ben didn't answer. He changed the subject, "It is a gorgeous sunset."
They watched the western sky until all light faded away.

# # # # #

Chapter 17

The Second Night

"It works." Danny held up Ben's radio. Any time he found something to prove his parents wrong, he announced it with great glee. That was particularly true of any errors his father made. He lifted the radio over his head and shook it trophy style. "What do you want to listen to, Dad?" Danny spun the tuner. Country stations, Spanish speaking broadcasts, and pop music floated over the campfire flames. The lantern had been turned off and the fire provided the campsite's only illumination. Even in that low light Ben could see the gloating smirk on his son's face.

"Bring it over here and I'll see what I can find." Ben extended his hand and motioned to his son. The boy scrambled out of his chair, squeezing dangerously close to the fire as he stepped between the blaze and his mother and Melanie. He handed the plastic box to Ben and said, "You're welcome." Ben made a disgusted grunt, shot him an evil stare, punched him in his arm lightly, and waved him back to his chair. Danny continued his circuit around the flames through what smoke the light breeze wafted into the dark skies.

"Don't turn it up too loud." Carolyn gestured to Melanie. The girl's chair was positioned as close to her mother's as possible. Melanie was draped over her mother's lap, sleeping peacefully. "She's out for the night." Carolyn caressed her daughter's hair gently.

Ben nodded and said, "Okay. How about some 70's and 80's rock?" He searched the radio for his oldies station, but after two unsuccessful trips up and down the dial, settled on a country and western station, playing an old Hank William's Sr. song. "Looks like we're stuck with music from the stone-age." He bent over to put the radio at his feet. As he did so, the pistol in his pants pocket pulled tight and reminded him of its presence.

"You like that kind of music, Ben." Carolyn said.

"Red-neck, red-neck, red-neck," Danny said in a sing-song voice. "Red-ass, red-ass, red-ass," Ben replied, "Is that what you want?"

Danny shook his head.

"So keep your comments to yourself." "Ben, was that necessary?" Carolyn asked.

"Yes." Ben's apprehension regarding what the coming night might bring was close to the surface. The littlest reminder rekindled the debate and started it replaying in his mind. Once ignited, it rolled over, and over, and over. What had he seen? Who or what caused it? Was he in danger? What should he do if…?" He had a frantic sense of urgency to avoid a reoccurrence. Panic was only an incident or a suggestion away from erupting. The tension made him overreact to most anything happening around him.

Carolyn shook her head and looked sad. She'd seen Ben be an absolute asshole before and he was giving signs he would surpass his previous performances.

The disk jockey announced to his audience they were listening to "Saturday Night Memories." The DJ spoke in a rural southern drawl that was so pronounced it made Ben wonder if the accent was faked. Even that minor issue evoked a response from Ben.

"Red-neck, my ass. I bet that spit-wad is from an Ivy League college, still wet-behind-the-ears, with his college communications diploma in his pocket," Ben said. He visualized a grad, in an Armani suit, fresh from a New England University, gloating as he faked his accent, sitting behind the radio mike. "Yes, that's phony," Ben decided after listening to a few more words. "You can bet he's a typical snob from some elite family in New York. They're all phony crap." Ben reasoned out loud, "Being phony is what it takes to get ahead now-days, I guess." Earl Scruggs's classic rendition of Foggy Mountain Breakdown came out of the speaker and Ben forgot the DJ. Scruggs's banjo work was always superb and he liked the number. He bent over again and turned up the volume

"Ben, please don't play it quite so loud," Carolyn repeated. Her look said "please" more fervently than the word. She glanced down at Melanie, explaining without uttering a word.

"Shit, Carolyn. It's not loud. If you're worried about her sleeping, put her ass in the damned tent." Ben looked at his watch. "It's past time for them to be in bed. Besides, you know Melanie." Their youngest daughter reduced the need for a clock in the evenings. The girl passed out promptly at 9:00 every night and attempts at rousing her normally proved unsuccessful.

"Okay... Okay." Carolyn eased out from underneath Melanie and helped her to her feet. Melanie stumbled along beside her mother in that child's world that lets them function half awake and half asleep. Big sister Angela's whining and complaints about having to turn off her radio, already so low it was barely audible, signaled Carolyn and Melanie's arrival at the children's tent. Within moments, Carolyn returned and all was quiet with the exception of Ben's radio. The children's tent was dark. Ben guessed both his daughters fell asleep within seconds of his wife's departure.

"When do you want to break camp tomorrow?" Carolyn picked up a stick and stood by the fire idly stirring the embers.

"Early. I want to get home before four," Ben said. "The earlier the better."

"Are we going fishing tomorrow?" Danny asked. "Haven't you had enough?" Ben replied.

"I never get enough fishing." Danny's ability to sit and watch a float for hours was legendary.

"Maybe for a couple hours after breakfast, but I figure we need to be headed back to the car by 11:00." Ben leaned back in his chair, stretched, and yawned. "I'm not promising." The lack of sleep from the night before was catching up with him, but Ben wondered if his nerves would keep him awake when he finally crawled in his sleeping bag.

"You and Danny go fishing. The girls and I will break camp and pack up. I've been cooped up in a canoe enough for this weekend." Carolyn sat down in her chair. "We'll have everything ready to go when you get back."

Ben nodded, mumbled "Okay," and stared into the fire. His mind wandered as weariness dulled his senses. Thoughts of the hallucinations from the prior evening passed through his mind and he immediately snapped his head up and peered into the darkness. Nothing was there. All Ben saw were a few clouds framing a tiny sliver of moon, stars dotting the remaining dark sky, and the emptiness of the vast grass prairie. His uneasiness kept him out of the tent and by the fire.

"Dad."

"Uh-huh."

"I have to take a leak." Danny still needed an escort at night. He hadn't completely shaken his childhood fear of the dark. This was doubly true when in strange surroundings.

"Come get the flashlight and go by yourself," Ben answered gruffly.

"I don't like going into the latrine at night with the canvas around it."

"Okay. Go piss in the creek." "Dad." Danny pleaded.

"When are you going to get over that?" Ben got to his feet and said, "Come on." He gently shoved Danny in the back with the flashlight registering his displeasure with the boy. After a couple steps he allowed the boy to get close to his side.

Ben's arm rubbed Danny's shoulder as they walked to the creek's edge. Father and son soon were adding to the depth of the stream. When they turned to return to the campfire, the flashlight's beam flickered then failed. Danny squealed and ran back to his chair while Ben stopped to fix the light.

Ben flicked the switch off and on, off and on. "Aww, crap. Those batteries are practically new." The bulb barely illuminated. It didn't seem reasonable for the batteries to have died instantly. He unscrewed the battery compartment lid and switched the battery's positions. That temporary fix worked for Ben a few times in the past. When he finished, the result was the same; the flashlight was dead. "Cheap Chinese junk. That's all you can buy anymore," Ben said, sighed, and started back to the fire. If they needed more light than the campfire provided he could light the lantern. Or get the kids' flashlight from their tent.

Before he covered a quarter of the distance to the fire, coldness brushed against his back and grasped him. The hair raised on his neck. He froze where his feet struck the ground. Turning his head slowly, Ben expected to see the same specter's eyes that watched, intimidated, and tortured his mind the prior night. His eyes swept the area behind him. There wasn't anything unusual; nothing was visible across the creek except empty prairie. No suspicious shadows lurked; everything was in its proper place. Nothing looked wrong…but, nothing felt right.

Another puff of cool February breeze buffed him. The nameless dread reinvaded Ben. Was the breath of wind that seemed to come from nowhere just nature or something more sinister? Ben's heart rate increased and panic made him turn completely around, slowly scanning the terrain surrounding him. Though his eyes saw nothing he could feel a presence. He started walking toward the fire, but quickly increased his speed to a trot.

# # # # #

Chapter   18

Ben stopped when he got to the fire. All thoughts and rationalization about the previous night's happenings being alcohol-induced hallucinations flew from his mind. He was convinced, without the inconvenience of reason, that something stalked him. It was out there waiting, Ben knew that. What stalked him, he wasn't sure. Ben's mind raced. The Indian? Yes, it was probably the Indian…or his people. Somehow the red man was orchestrating the whole thing. That was the most logical explanation. The Indian used lasers or something else Ben didn't understand to create the illusions. The bastard was an engineer. It had to be— the other possibility was far more frightening. If it wasn't the Indian, the only thing left was a supernatural event which he would be powerless against. He didn't want that!

Where was it? Ben circled the fire looking away from the flames, disregarding the stares of his wife and son. Nothing. Nothing. Nothing. He was oblivious of everything except the dark emptiness surrounding the camp. Something lurked in the blackness, he was sure, but he couldn't find it. All possibility that what had happened last night were hallucinations were dead—he knew otherwise. As he made his second circle around the fire, Carolyn's voice broke through his self-induced trance. "Ben... Ben... Ben... What on earth are you doing? Ben?"

"Nothing." Ben took a last glance around the camp's perimeter, stepped back to his chair, and sat down cautiously. He was so focused on the danger somewhere in the dark he was unaware of the alarm his strange actions produced in Carolyn and Danny.

"What's going on?" Carolyn's concern rapidly became fear. Her husband's behavior was unexplainable. "You're scaring me."

"Nothing," Ben repeated. He shot an angry glance at her.

"Is something out there, Daddy?" Danny sounded frightened. "No, damn it, no!" Ben said sharply. "Can't I just check around the camp without everyone going nuts?" He looked at his son's face. It was distorted with wide-eyed fear. Ben lashed out because he couldn't think of what he should do. "There's nothing out there. You need to go to the tent and get some sleep. Damn, boy, are we going to have to put you back in diapers?" Ben pointed to Danny then to the children's tent, peering behind it for an instant, in case...

"Go with me," Danny said.

"I'll go with you." Carolyn stood and waited for her boy. She looked at her husband with disgust and contempt. "He's scared, Ben."

"That boy has got to grow up," Ben snapped. His bluster covered his fears and hid them from Carolyn and Danny…he hoped.

Carolyn looked back at Ben and said bitterly, "Not tonight."

Ben could hear Carolyn talking to Danny as they entered the tent. Her words and tone were reassuring. Danny stayed silent, evidently soothed by Carolyn's presence.

Ben's neck swiveled as he made another quick survey around the camp. Nothing was visible. There wasn't a single sign of any human presence. Still, the feeling of foreboding pressed him. His mind leaped to what the alternatives might be if the Indian wasn't causing the mischief. As quickly as Ben reopened the thought process, suggesting the things happening to him were products of his brain, he dismissed it. To manufacture something like this in his mind would mean he would have to be insane. Never. That couldn't be. His thoughts turned to the supernatural.

Could what the Indian said be true? Was this a place no one should go? Ben's sense of reason rebelled at such a notion. Life wasn't a TV series like something on the Science Fiction Channel, or the Twilight Zone, or Outer Limits. But, if he was sane, and he was sure of that, and it wasn't the Indian or his operatives, what other possibility was there? If the presence of evil existed at this place, what could he do? What form would it take? What would it do to him? The eyes he'd seen had to be housed in a huge creature. Would it attack and carry him off to the Hell he'd learned about in childhood? Would it crash down on him like some horrible monster from Jurassic Park, tearing his body to shreds with its claws, crushing his skull with its jaws, and ripping his flesh from his bones? He saw this vision clearly. The beast stood over a pile of bones and bloody gore that had been his body. Ben frantically resumed his visual search around the camp.

Not a single sign of trouble appeared no matter how hard he strained his eyes. He slowly realized there wasn't anything spying on the camp. Not right then. He began to feel foolish.

"What's going on?" Carolyn stood by her chair with a questioning look on her face. Ben didn't even know she'd returned from the tent. Her voice jerked him away from his search and out of his conjectures.

"Nothing."

"Bull-shit, Ben. You're acting strange. Really strange. What in the hell is going on?"

"Christ, Carolyn! It's nothing. I just thought I saw some animals moving around." Ben looked away from her. Carolyn could look into his eyes and know when he was lying.

"You're making me very nervous. Ben, is something... Are you sure you're all right?"

"I'm okay." Ben stood up and walked to the firewood pile, picked some wood up, and tossed a couple of logs on the fire before returning to his chair. He stood by the canvas and aluminum seat searching the vacant grasslands.

Carolyn looked at him, skepticism showing in her eyes. "If there is something wrong, tell me. Maybe I can help."

"Damn, just leave me alone." Ben bent over and turned the volume up on the radio. He straightened up and looked at Carolyn with a defiant scowl before dropping into his chair.

She shook her head and stared into the flames. Carolyn mumbled, "I tried." Being married to Ben was frustrating.

Carolyn and Ben sat by the fire, their thoughts in two very different worlds. Ben's were for his safety and what his family could do to escape if the specter came after him. Would this malevolent specter attack them, too? Did evil live in him? One of them? If so, who would it attack first? What would his family think of him if they learned of his suspicions? Could he escape if the beast raged through their camp?

Carolyn's thoughts and concerns were for her husband's mental state and health. Was he likely to hurt himself? Her, or the kids? Should she find the cell phone just in case? How could she give someone directions if she needed help? How would they be able to reach them?

They sat, half listening to the music playing on the radio, staring into the fire, their minds detached from each other. Block by block an invisible wall was being erected between the two and it kept them from communicating.

Ben couldn't stop from making his quick visual checks around the camp. None of these peeks disclosed a thing, but his feeling of uneasiness didn't lessen. He felt small needles prick his skin in thousands of places over his back, arms, and neck as the nebulous fear kept Ben sitting at the fire. His breathing was shallow and hurried. Frozen statue-like, he avoided any movement that might draw the attention of the nameless, shapeless dread. Carolyn stubbornly stayed next to him because she sensed she might be needed, though that sense was based more on intuition than observing the visible signs of Ben's distress she clearly read.

Nothing happened. More minutes passed. There were still no threatening signs. A half-hour passed. There wasn't any danger, Ben had just panicked. He relaxed a bit and some of the stress left his face.

"You feel a little better?" Carolyn asked.

"I didn't feel bad, Carolyn." He looked sheepish. "I thought the Indian might be snooping around. Maybe I saw something, maybe I didn't. It's gone, I guess. I didn't want to scare you." He was careful not to look at her. "You ever just get a feeling and you let it get to you?"

"Oh, yes," she said.

"Well, that's what happened—let's just let it go. We need to concentrate on something else. They're playing some good songs on the radio. What do you say?" He leaned back in his chair, sighed, and tried to relax.

"Okay. I like what they're playing. But Ben, let me know what's going on with you. And if you do see something, tell me."

He nodded.

The radio played music that included bluegrass performers, 'Grand Old Opry' stars, and country classics. Some individuals Ben didn't recognize. Bill Monroe, Earnest Tubb, Red Foley, Kitty Wells, Ralph Stanley, and others were before his time, but songs by Merle Haggard, Faith Hill, George Jones, Alan Jackson, and Taylor Swift... they were familiar. As those songs played, Ben's fear lessened. He made a conscious effort to refocus his attention. Listening to tunes he knew, ones his father knew, reassured him his world remained intact. Maybe if he buried his head in the sands of music coming from the plastic box, his fears might go away. An hour passed. He relaxed more and more. So did Carolyn.

The line-up of Ben's favorite old-time country singers continued. Brenda Lee sang "I'm Sorry." Carolyn started to hum along with the radio. She said, "I always liked her. I wonder if she's still entertaining."

"Don't know," Ben said.

"My mom and dad always used to listen to country music. They went to Nashville a couple times. Maybe we could go there or Dollywood—or maybe go to some concerts. I'd like to see Brad Paisley or Keith Urban."

"Uh-huh." Ben stared into the fire semi-ignoring his wife.

"I think there's a couple shows coming to the area. One in Naples that's bluegrass and there's one in Tampa. I think Reba will be there. Which would you like to go to?"

"Uh-huh." Ben was rebuffing Carolyn's obvious attempt to start a conversation. She became silent.

Both Ben and Carolyn fell deeper into their separate worlds. Alan Jackson sang about it being five o'clock somewhere. Dolly Parton sang about working nine to five. Though physically, Carolyn sat two feet from Ben's side, at that moment the emotional gulf between them was miles wide. Her eyes narrowed as sleep tempted them.

Conway Twitty crooned, "I'm lying here with Linda on my mind." As the recording played, the disc jockey began singing along with Conway. After the first verse, it evolved into a not too harmonic duet. The DJ's singing voice sounded different than when he announced, but somehow familiar. Ben ignored that until the song's refrain when the disk jockey substituted the name Carolyn for Linda. Gradually the DJ's voice dominated and Conway's faded to silence. Ben knew that voice, but... When the song repeated the refrain and 'Carolyn' was inserted again, Ben sat up in shock and stared at the radio. It was Bill Miller's voice! Dead Bill Miller!

Ben kicked the radio viciously. The song continued. He yelled, "Bastard," rose from his chair, and kicked the black plastic box again.

"What are you doing? What's wrong?" Carolyn was standing, eyes wide with alarm. The firelight dancing on her face made her look twice as frightened, twice as shocked.

"That! Hear that bastard? That Son-of-a-bitch." Ben pointed to the radio.

"What? You like Conway Twitty." Carolyn looked confused.

The song ended and Miller's voice went silent. The next sound from the radio was the announcer telling his listeners the news followed. Ben peered at the radio. What was happening? He heard Carolyn calling his name from a far off distance, saying words he refused to hear. Did he have a dream, a nightmare? That was it. He'd dozed off and the last two days' tension and revelations invaded his sleep. It was a nightmare. It had to be. But it didn't feel like one. Carolyn was shaking his arm, forcing him to pay attention to her.

"Are you okay? Ben? For God's sake, what's happening with you? Are you okay?" Her voice trembled.

Ben shook his head, trying to remove the cobwebs of what must be sleep from his mind...his mind that must have created the nightmare. Carolyn's face was concerned and very frightened.

Ben said, "Yeah. I must have fallen asleep and had a dream. In my dream Bill Miller was singing on the radio."

Carolyn looked exasperated and relieved at the same time. "That man is just like a bad penny that keeps coming back." She shook her head. "I think the old saying from that play is very true. Forget you ever knew that worthless—"

"What's that?" Ben asked. He wanted his mind to concentrate on anything but his fears.

"What's what?"

"The old saying? I don't know what you're talking about."

"Oh. I read it in a book, I think." Carolyn thought for a second. "Shakespeare. Julius Caesar, maybe. It goes something like, 'a man's evil lives after him, while his good is buried with his bones.' I don't remember exactly."

"'The good is oft times interred with his bones.' Yes, I remember that from somewhere. Might have been Shakespeare." Ben looked around the camp's perimeter uneasily. The reference to evil in Carolyn's quote reawakened his preoccupation with the unknown entity.

"Don't you think we should go to bed?" Carolyn suggested. "You're falling asleep out here." Though her words didn't, her eyes pleaded.

Ben thought for a few seconds before answering. He would like to go to the tent, pull the sleeping bag over his head, and hide from what threatened him. But, something within him would not allow that. Fear of being unprepared for some assault... A morbid fascination with the frightful events that were pursuing him... Perhaps both formed his decision. "I want to stay up a little while longer. You go to bed if you want."

"No. I'm going to stay up with you." Carolyn saw the nervous, worried look on Ben's face. She grimly resolved to sit by the fire until he battled and defeated the problem or demon she knew struggled within him. Carolyn couldn't hurry Ben to the comforting haven of the tent; she knew that. He'd have to make that decision.

The breeze had changed slightly and Ben's chair was in the smoke. Carolyn moved both their chairs out of its drift. Ben nodded his thanks and they both sat down to watch the fire. Her hand sought his. Carolyn intertwined their fingers as she grasped and squeezed his hand.

# # # # #

Chapter   19

The Way Out

The bright Florida morning sunlight and warm breeze did little to affect the chill that settled on the camp, a chill not caused by brisk February temperatures, but by the night's bizarre happenings. No one rose early. Ben and Carolyn's meager slumber was troubled by thoughts and questions, though very different in character that rambled through their minds. They both fell into a deep exhausted sleep a couple hours before dawn. When they did wake, the sun was above the eastern tree line by several degrees. Other than the obligatory, "Good morning," "How are you?" and one word answers, both dressed in silence. They tried, but failed to find words that would make sense of the previous night. Those words didn't exist. Conversation that took place was spawned by necessity and avoided the issues clawing at their minds.

Carolyn was the first to leave the tent. She hesitated as she stepped through the opening. "I think we should leave after breakfast, don't you?" she said.

It wasn't a question, but Ben answered, "Yes."

Ben listened for the normal bickering and banter between the children. It was non-existent. They stayed in their tent and spoke in hushed tones. Rock music playing on Angela's radio provided the only normal noise coming from the three. The children didn't leave their canvas haven until after Carolyn's signal. They weren't sure if they were safe and not sure of what their father's actions might be.

Danny asked his mother, "Are we going to fish today?" "Not today, we need to get home," She answered. "Aww, mom, just for a little while?"

"Sorry, we're going straight back to the car after breakfast." Carolyn's answers to her son's questions were spoken loud enough to be sure her husband heard them. It was a message to Ben, to which Angela decided to add one of her own.

"Danny, you and Melanie need to keep your voices down and stay out of trouble. Dad might be hung over. It sounded like he got bombed last night." Angela made her comments loud enough so the alligators that cruised the creek could hear.

Angela guessed, incorrectly, that her father had been "hitting the bottle," causing the commotion and upset, waking the children, and scaring them. She expressed her thoughts to the young ones, lessening their confusion, if not their concerns. It was the teenager's way of rebuking her parent, for her loud delivery was intended to make sure Ben would hear. She expected him or her mother to shout something at her, but when he didn't and Carolyn remained silent, it bothered her more than if they had. The children knew something was seriously wrong. All three moved about the camp cautiously, taking pains to be helpful and not to do anything to upset their parents.

As was often the case, Ben's thoughts went to considering changing his behavior after it created a near-disaster in his life. He pulled on his trousers and shirt, thinking maybe it was time to give more weight to religion. When he got out of this mess… Yes, he'd think about that…later. Later was okay because he told himself God was forgiving and he could seek forgiveness…later.

Ben fiddled around inside the tent, postponing the smothering embarrassment his actions the night before would bring when he faced his family. He finally emerged from hiding into the cool February air and ignored their stares. Ben tried to act as if nothing had transpired, that all was normal. His performance lacked conviction for his confidence was eroded to its core. Other than obligatory "good mornings," there was no conversation, no questions, no communication with his family; unless the cautious and unsure stares his children fastened on him when he wasn't looking at them were considered.

Ben scratched around in the campfire ashes and rekindled the flames by tossing on a few slivers of lighter pine. Keeping a fire burning morning and evening was part of Ben's ritual. The need to rekindle it was secondary. The flames familiar sight, smell, and sound were especially important this morning. Performing the routine soothed him and helped isolate him from his problems and, unusually, from his family. The fire normally drew the children to it like a magnet, but not this morning. He was glad of that.

As he fussed with the burning logs, he heard Carolyn at the stove clinking her skillets and pots. Soon the smell of bacon and eggs joined that of percolating coffee. Ben pulled his chair up to the awakening flames, sat close to them, staring into the fire, his mind still fogged and confused with the last two nights' occurrences. Carolyn touched him lightly on the back. "Here's a cup of coffee." She stood back a little distance to see if Ben reacted adversely to her touch.

"Thanks." Ben looked at Carolyn's face. Her lip was still swollen. "You know I didn't mean to do that." He stood half-way, reached out gently and touched her mouth. Her body stiffened at his finger's contact. Ben eased back into his chair.

"I know you wouldn't do it intentionally." Ben noticed the lack of surety in Carolyn's words as she handed him the coffee. "I still don't know what was happening to you. It was like you weren't... you just weren't right. You weren't you."

Ben took a sip of coffee. "I wish I could explain it to you. Hell, I wish I could explain it to myself." He shook his head. "Everything seemed so real. I thought you were seeing what I saw. And the radio. Crazy stuff was coming out of it. It was…there were people laughing. And stuff got said. Miller again. And I saw those eyes…I just can't believe all that was an illusion. You didn't see or hear anything?"

Carolyn shook her head. "No. Nothing." She gently rubbed her lower lip. "You're tired. That's all." Carolyn reached over and rubbed his shoulder. "Are you going to tell me more about what you saw? You just said eyes." She stepped closer to him.

Ben hesitated, then said, "Sure." He tried to think of ways to describe what his eyes saw or his mind conjured. It was so real to him. "I know this sounds crazy. There were two huge eyes looking at me. I couldn't make out the shape of an animal or anything they were contained in." He hesitated to see Carolyn's reaction. It was concern. "They were as large as soccer balls. I swear. The colors in the irises kept changing: maroon, violet, and crimson, real weird looking. The whites...you could see blood vessels in them. But the main thing was how angry they looked. It was like pure hate was coming out of them."

Carolyn was wide-eyed. "How close did you think they were? Did they come after you?"

"They didn't move. I guess they were about twenty feet away." Ben looked at the prairie. He felt very foolish telling her his fantasy. "It sounds stupid, I know that. Crazy for sure. You must have thought that watching me. I guess what the Indian told us worked on me more than I could have ever imagined."

"You mean his story about the dead chief being buried here and this being a place no one should go?" Carolyn asked.

"Yeah, and about this being a spot that is only safe for people who aren't evil." Ben tried to suck his words back in but it was too late.

A strange look formed on her face. Carolyn stared at him for several seconds before saying, "Are you afraid there is evil in you?"

Ben was silent, thinking of how to answer. He told himself he wasn't, but was that enough? Was he right? Was he honest with himself? "I…don't really believe I'm evil." The hesitation said more than the words.

"Ben, maybe…," Carolyn paused before carefully wording her response. "It could be you have doubts. Those doubts are bothering you. The Indian made you look at them. Maybe you have to admit them to yourself. Maybe you ha…," The coffee pot on the Coleman stove boiled over causing blue flames to flare into yellows and make a loud hissing sound. Carolyn said, "Oh!" and ran to the stove to set the coffee off.

The children approached, ending further discussion on the subject. Adults and children focused on breakfast.

# # # # #

Chapter   20

"That should do it." Ben checked the position of the camping gear in the canoes. To say that the camp tear down had been hasty was a giant understatement. An example was the Coleman stove that was still warm enough to cause Ben to drop it twice when carrying it to the creek's edge.

"You don't want us to put the stuff in our canoe in plastic bags?" Angela asked.

"I don't think it's necessary," Ben said.

Angela rolled her eyes and smirked, but kept her mouth shut. "Are you going to take one quick look around the site?" Carolyn asked Ben.

"A real quick one." He walked a few steps up the bank, saw that the water used to dowse the fire had done its job, swiveled his head back and forth quickly and said, "We're ready."

The whole family participated with a sense of urgency as they loaded the canoes fast. There was good reason for hurrying back to the car and home, all sensed they needed to get away from the unfriendly piece of ground on which they had intruded.

No one spoke of what happened the previous night, except Melanie who asked. "Why did daddy shoot the gun last night?"

That question and others that might have been ventured were quickly silenced by her mother, "We aren't going to talk at all about what happened last night today, sweetie. Maybe we will tomorrow." The Callison children understood Carolyn was speaking to them all.

Within two hours of finishing breakfast, Ben, Carolyn, and their kids pushed their heavily laden canoes off the creek bank. The children looked back at the campsite as they paddled, following their parents' canoe down the creek. Ben and Carolyn did not.

The current flowed in the direction they traveled on the return trip. Minutes into their voyage back to the car it was apparent they'd have little to do but gently dip their paddles and steer. Ben relaxed some, relieved he'd escaped the mound of dirt that wanted to claim him. Not Carolyn, who was anxious and jumpy. She kept peering at the creek's entrance into the cypress swamp. Occasionally, she stopped paddling and concentrated on the opening. The stream's serpentine curves kept them from seeing deep into the trees. Though he knew she was still deeply troubled by his actions, Ben guessed where Carolyn's mind was focused and what was creating her agitation. "Worried about going under that tree?" he asked.

"Yes." Carolyn didn't look around.

"The chance of another snake…being in the same spot…just as we go under…that's a million to one shot." Ben tried his best to sound reassuring.

"The way things have gone this weekend, it will be that one." Carolyn continued to stare at the opening.

Ben started to say something to reassure her no moccasin waited for them, but decided against belaboring the subject. His credibility was at its lowest ebb. And there was no reason to create additional tension. Just in case, he asked, "Where did you pack the gun?"

Carolyn remained silent.

"Is the pistol in one of the duffle bags?"

"I have it," Carolyn answered.

"Hand it on back to me," Ben said.

"No."

"Hand it back."

"No."

"Hand it back. I need to reload it with snake shot," Ben demanded in an exasperated voice.

Carolyn looked back at him. "I've already reloaded the gun." She paused and when she continued there was no negotiation in her tone. "I'm going to keep the gun. We have a lot to sort out. You need to go to the doctor. I know how to use the pistol and I believe we'll all be safer if I keep it." Carolyn's eyes bored into Ben's.

Ben shrugged his shoulders and said, "Okay. After last night— well, I understand."

Carolyn continued to look at him as though she expected him to do or say something.

Her look made Ben uncomfortable. He looked past Carolyn to break her penetrating gaze. "You won't have to worry about a snake on the tree." His voice was grim and his eyes were fixed on something in front of them.

Carolyn turned to see what Ben watched downstream. He was looking down the creek into the swamp. Two thirds of the fallen tree stretching across the creek was visible. Right in the middle of the span, a man sat with his back to them. Carolyn gasped. Unless others had an identical shirt, the man sitting on the log was the Indian who visited their campsite and dramatically impacted their lives. He'd never threatened them in a direct way, but Carolyn and Ben both believed he had some connection with their ordeal. "What do we do?" Carolyn whispered.

"Nothing. We have to go under there to get back." Ben thought for a second or two. "Let's have the kids go through first so we can watch him and be sure they get through alright."

"We can't do that!"

"Look. If we go first and something happens to us, the kids are helpless. We're in a better position to protect them if we're behind. Besides, I don't think he's going to do anything." Ben held his hand toward Carolyn. "Are you sure you want to keep the revolver?"

Carolyn sat like a statue for several seconds. She finally nodded and said, "I'll keep the gun," reluctantly confirming the depth of her concern about Ben's mental condition.

They were close enough to see the Indian's boots dangling beneath the far side of the tree. The canoes would have to pass within ten feet of the man.

Ben waved to Angela and called, "You go first." He sculled against the current to keep the canoe in position while the children's boat passed. Angela looked nervous as she pulled along side her parents. "You sure you want us to go first?" Angela asked.

"Yes. It should be easy, you're heading downstream. We can watch so if you do get into trouble, get wedged underneath, something like that, it's easier to assist from this side. Don't worry. It's easier to go with the current. Stay as close to the shore as you can. It'll be a piece of cake." Ben said.

"What about?" Angela pointed her paddle at the Indian. Danny and Melanie were wild-eyed and stunned to silence.

"You'll be fine," her mother said. "Just get under and keep going." Carolyn tried to sound calm and reassuring.

Ben let the children get eighty feet ahead before saying, "Okay," to Carolyn. They resumed paddling, being sure they maintained the distance as a reaction cushion between the two canoes.

He repeated in a whisper, "Do you want me to take the gun?" Without looking back, Carolyn shook her head hard. She glanced at something in front of her seat, moved it with her foot, its movement making a metallic scraping noise.

The Indian's jet-black hair glistened in the light. They could see the red bandana tied around his neck covering all the skin between his collar and hair. As far as Ben could tell, the man took no notice of them, though Angela's verbal canoe handling instructions to Danny and Melanie had to be audible to him. He remained still as a statue. The man didn't have any fishing lines in the water; he was just sitting, looking down the stream.

Danny and Melanie flattened down into the canoe to pass under the tree as Angela maneuvered the boat close to shore and through the only place the canoe could pass. Ben watched Angela bend forward and down as she glided under the log. The children and the Indian exchanged 'Hello's' as their canoe continued down the creek.

Ben concentrated on controlling the canoe as they neared the cypress. He glanced at Carolyn who leaned forward to create clearance between her and the tree. Ben noticed something clutched in her right hand... it was his gun. The Indian never changed his position on the log. His back was still to them though Ben could have reached out with the paddle and touched the man's jeans. Ben made a quick move downward to clear the tree as he glided forward. For a split second, all he could see was the canoe's bottom and the green duffle bags packed at his feet as he passed under the cypress. The canoe came within a few feet of the Indian's boots. Ben wasn't sure if the few seconds of coolness was shade from the tree or...

Ben straightened back up and turned to look at the Indian in one motion. The man stared back at him impassively, nodded and said, "Hello."

"Hello," Ben answered. "It's a nice day."

"Very nice." The Indian did not change his expression. Ben back paddled a little. He didn't want to let the red bastard know he was intimidated. That was important. Ben looked the man in his dark brown eyes. The Indian returned his gaze, dispassionately focused on Ben's light blue-gray pupils. The man's face had an ageless quality about it. He could have been thirty or fifty-five.

Though Carolyn had told him she hadn't seen what horrified him the previous night, Ben could not resist the temptation to see if the Indian was involved in some way. Maybe he'd disclose evidence about a part he might have played in the past two nights' terrifying events.

"That's a nice camping spot." Ben attempted to keep his voice calm and poised, but a little nervous edge crept into its tone. "What's supposed to happen to people who stay there?"

"Nothing you would care to know, since what you say tells me nothing happened to you." The Indian's expression stayed the same despite his inflection on the word 'say.'

"I'm curious. What is supposed to happen? Does somebody or something come after you? Maybe take your scalp?" Ben's tone was as sarcastic as his words.

The Indian's expression remained the same. His bronze left hand moved toward his body. "Nothing happens to them here or here," the man said, first touching his heart, then drawing his index finger across his throat. "It happens here," pointing to his eyes with his index and middle fingers, "and here," making a fist and tapping his head. "I am glad nothing happened to you." The Indian returned Ben's sarcasm. "You are welcome to return anytime you are willing."

"Let's go," Carolyn's voice pleaded. "Just a min… "

"No. I want to go now. The kids are getting too far ahead of us." Carolyn was firm as she cut Ben off.

"Some other time," Ben said. The Indian nodded stonily.

Ben waved the paddle at the Indian, then turned and stroked fast enough to catch the children's canoe. Before they reached the creek's next curve Ben looked back for a last glimpse of the Indian, but the man had disappeared.

# # # # #

Chapter 21

A Place No One Can Return From

"What's wrong with this damn TV, Carolyn?" Ben said as he mashed buttons on the remote.

Carolyn's voice came from the kitchen, "I was just watching it a little while ago. It was fine."

"It won't change stations." Ben began cursing.

"Calm down, Ben. Have you got the right remote?"

He looked at the device in his hand. "Shit!" Ben snatched up the proper remote from the coffee table and tossed the other one aside.

"That take care of it?" Carolyn gloated from afar.

"Yes," Ben added, bitch, under his breath. He was still a little up tight from the effects of their camping trip. The television screen changed pictures as Ben mashed the remote's buttons. He switched between ESPN and other cable channels each time the basketball game was interrupted by a commercial. Holding the remote, he felt in control. Ben needed to regain the feeling. He'd had so little in the past seventy-two hours. His mind wandered.

After passing under the cypress and their encounter with the Seminole, the rest of the canoe trip, loading the car, and the ride home, proved uneventful. While driving the car, most of the tension drained from him and, he hoped, the family. Most, not all.

The first thing that had disappeared from his mind was his decision to consider changing his life-style. He was home, the danger far away. Later was all he addressed. Any change would come much, much…later. Though he could dismiss altering his behavior until…later, he couldn't dismiss his guilt.

His youngest children were willing to forget the trip's unusual happenings and their father's strange behavior. They quickly became engaged in their normal arguing and antagonizing. Angela had stared at him questioningly for a while, but quickly went back to her normal behavior, ignoring his presence when the phone started to ring and she reentered her social whirl. Evidently, she'd decided that any fears she had weren't worth the worry. But Carolyn…Carolyn was quiet; that bothered him.

When the last canoe was secured to the top of his SUV, Ben was ready to return to life as it had been when he'd unloaded it three days before. Driving home physically transported him from the fantasy Never-Never land to which he vowed he'd never return, back to his world, back to things the way they were. Ben was ready to ignore the whole bizarre episode. He was able to, though he knew only temporarily. For fleeting seconds, his thoughts would wander back to the prior night's bizarre visions. He forced his mind to focus on other things when this happened.

Ben repeatedly wrestled with the thought that evil might reside in him. It wouldn't go away, shoving back into his thoughts as he tried to justify his value system. It took different forms including flashbacks. He remembered a conversation he had with his mother as an adolescent. He could see her face as she said, "Benjamin, the school called. We have to talk about it."

"What's wrong?" He acted innocent, but knew it was about cheating on his school work.

"Sister Mary Alice told me she took the copy of the answer sheets you smuggled into her class. You were cheating! You know that. Why would you do such a thing?"

"That wasn't true. Those were my study notes. I didn't realize my notebook was open. It fell on the floor and just opened to that page." Ben looked away as he told his lie.

"Look at me, Benny, dear." He did.

"Oh, Benny, you're lying! I can see it in your eyes."

"It's your fault! You and Dad are always on my back to get A's. I   wouldn't have to cheat otherwise."

"Benny, Benny, Benny. You just made the bad thing you did evil. You lied! You told me you didn't cheat when you know you did. You can't get away with that. Even if Sister didn't see you and I didn't know you lied, God sees you. His eyes can see right into your heart. You don't want to be a son of the devil do you?"

He answered, "No, mama," and felt bad, but for getting caught, not for the act. Still, Ben's mother's words had their effect. He often wondered if he was evil in his mother's judgment and if that made him a "son of the devil."

Ben mentally argued the things men like Bundy and Dahmer did were evil. Not the things he did. Not in his peers' judgment. Ben told himself he was not evil. Tilting business odds in his favor by telling a lie or two, or a little "action" on the side weren't vile. Most people he knew, even Presidents, did that. Clinton, Bush, and Obama were all evil by his mother's standards. Still…the weekend exhumed the question he kept buried. It was a query that he couldn't permanently answer and which wouldn't leave his mind. He thumped the palm of his hand on the steering wheel and said aloud, "Not me."

"What?" Carolyn asked. She looked at him questioningly. "Oh, nothing. Just some work stuff."

Carolyn didn't say anything, but her eyes told him she didn't believe him. He forced his attention back to his driving and he avoided looking at her for the remainder of the silent ride.

When they reached home, Ben made a relieved sigh when his foot touched his driveway's pavement. He was on his turf, secure again. "The place no one should go" was far away. Whatever terror, spirits, or magic the spot contained were there, not in his safe, familiar house. Ben felt sure his hallucinations were over and life would go on as though he'd never been on the camping trip. When he dismissed his fears, thoughts about the morality of his actions were easier to abandon. By the time the car was unpacked, he told himself he'd deal with his feelings of guilt again the next time he cheated on Carolyn or did something shady at work, for Ben freely admitted to himself he would in all likelihood do these actions.

As they lifted the canoe from the car, a cool zephyr blew against his neck and he swiveled around, almost dropping the canoe. Carolyn and Angela struggled but maintained control of the hull. Carolyn said, "What are you doing?"

Ben laughed wryly. "Sorry, I got a crink in my neck." The residual jumpiness from the weekend hadn't left.

Ben's major remaining concern was Carolyn. She watched him continuously on the drive home and he caught her frowning at him several times. He'd noticed she was quieter than usual and avoided being alone with him since their arrival home. It confirmed his suspicion that she was very upset. That was the way his wife dealt with her serious problems. She hated confrontation and conflict, particularly with Ben. When she was ready, she'd make her well thought out arguments in a conciliatory, but persistent manner. Getting hit in the face and witnessing him blast away at an invisible enemy would qualify as a serious problem he grimly agreed.

After dinner, when the children had left the table, Carolyn asked, "Ben, don't you feel it would be good for you to see a doctor?"

"No," he said.

"What would it hurt? If nothing is wrong, we can all laugh about it. If there is, you'll get help."

"Don't make a bigger thing out of this weekend than it was. Hey, I'm back home, I'm alright, let's get on with our lives." Ben knew she would continue to try to persuade him. He was equally determined to continue to deny any need.

"Ben, you can't just ignore what you did on the camping trip. I'm going to make you an appointment with Dr. Sterling, okay?"

"Can you give me a couple days to see how I am?" Ben asked.

"No!" Carolyn was emphatic.

"Okay, I guess I'll go." Ben was shocked by her strong response, but had no intention of seeing a shrink. Carolyn was upset and she had a right to be. However, Ben was sure a couple days of normal behavior would put her mind at ease. The appointment would just go away.

# # # # #

Chapter   22

After supper, the day wound down. Melanie and Danny took early baths, crawled sleepily into familiar beds, and allowed slumber to replenish their youthful vigor a couple of days in the outdoors claimed. Angela was still bouncing around the house, talking on the telephone, catching up on the weekend's gossip from her classmates. Ben knew she wouldn't get off and stay off the phone until he or Carolyn made her.

Carolyn kept herself busy rather than relaxing with a book or watching television with Ben as she usually did after weekend outings. He knew she washed a couple loads of laundry and ran the vacuum cleaner over floors that did not need the attention. Carolyn's activity confirmed Ben's fear the weekend's unsettling events weren't going to fade quickly. She always immersed herself in work or some similar isolating diversion when something bothered her.

His daughter interrupted his musings. Angela wandered into the living room to see what television program Ben was watching. She pressed her cell phone against her ear with her shoulder while she carried a bowl of ice cream in one hand and a spoon in the other. When she saw the basketball game, she said, "Gross," under her breath. She was in her nightgown, a filmy creation that covered her breasts and panties, but clearly revealed her body. Angela dropped the phone. She bent over to pick it up and Ben couldn't help thinking his daughter was going to be one sexy woman in a few years.

Ben looked at his watch. It was 10:15; time to put an end to Angela's phone sessions for the night. "Okay, princess. You're fifteen minutes past phone curfew. Say your goodbyes. Tomorrow's a school day."

"I have to go, the phone police are after me. See you tomorrow." Angela made a face at her father as she left the room. He heard Carolyn scolding her daughter as they passed, telling Angela, "You know you can't walk around that way. Your brother has his friends here all the time."

Carolyn sat down on the couch next to her husband, but at the opposite end. "Ben, I wish you would talk to her about that. Angela won't listen to me as long as you condone her walking around in her nightgown or underwear. She's not a little girl any more."

Ben grinned, "She's going to be a sexy broad like her mother." He reached over and grabbed her thigh.

Carolyn pushed his hand away angrily. "This is serious. She shouldn't be parading in front of Danny and you. She has about as much shame as a stripper."

"I understand those girls make a lot of money," Ben said jokingly.

"I'm going to bed!" Carolyn angrily sprang up off the couch. She frowned at Ben and said, "Don't wake me when you come in."

Ben realized he'd made a mistake and called out, "Okay, I'll talk to her," as Carolyn left the room. Carolyn was even more upset than he judged. An exchange like that wouldn't normally have caused her to do anything except roll her eyes. Certainly, it wouldn't have produced the anger evident in her features and voice. He thought about apologizing, but decided it wouldn't do any good. Besides, Ben saw that kind of apology as a sign of weakness and he rationalized he didn't have anything to apologize for.

He watched the game for another quarter hour. One team was so far ahead that viewing any longer was pointless. Ben clicked his way through the cable channels, stopping a few seconds at each. A segment of Howard Stern's show caught his eye and he watched it for ten minutes before deciding the only reason the girl was being interviewed were two melon-sized breasts she was willing to bare on TV. He never considered that those bare breasts were what caused him to pause there. Ben flashed through a few more stations before checking his watch. It was almost 11:00, time to go to bed.

As he turned off the TV, he asked the empty room, "Anything else before I hit the sack?" The children, under Angela's supervision, were supposed to have stored the camping equipment in the garage and the utility shed. Ben decided he better check on their efforts. The kids left camping equipment in the yard after one recent trip and neighborhood dogs had destroyed two sleeping bags as a result. A cold brisk wind struck him in the face when he opened the front door. He shivered a little, but decided he didn't need a jacket for the brief period he'd be outside. The place where the equipment had been piled was empty. Ben nodded his approval to the wind; the children even locked the storage shed. The canoes rested on their racks, the paddles properly stowed. Any items that might be damaged by marauding hounds were safe.

Ben shook as he walked, but not from the cool air. Seeing the canoes rekindled the previous night's memories. With each step the familiar dread increased in his consciousness. He stopped a few feet from his front door. The urge to turn around, to see if anything was behind him, became intense. But…the fear he'd be confronted by those malevolent eyes or some other terror his mind might create, kept him from doing so. Ben took the last few steps to the door. As he grasped the latch, a sensation like icy fingers touching both sides of his face caused him to flinch. He pulled the door open, dashed through, slamming and locking it behind him. The cold grip didn't follow. Ben wanted to peek out the window to see if his fears were true. He couldn't force himself to look. His hands were shaking. This is just in my mind!

Ben carried that thought as he turned out lights and carefully avoided looking outside. His nightly responsibilities were completed with shivering hands and body before he made his way to Carolyn and his room.

The bedroom door was closed. Ben hesitated a second to regain his composure before entering the room. Since sex was out of the question, he wanted to be sure he didn't wake Carolyn. No sense making things worse. His hand stopped shaking as he turned the doorknob. A low moan came from inside the room. He stood frozen by fear. What was happening behind the door? The moaning was repeated, this time louder and longer. It was definitely Carolyn making the sounds. Did some interloper have her? Had the nameless specter invaded the house? His shotguns were inside the bedroom closet and he didn't know what Carolyn had done with his pistol.

He put his ear to the door. The moaning continued. It didn't sound as though she was in pain. It sounded as though she was... Ben yanked the door open and stepped into the bedroom. What he saw on the bed paralyzed him. Carolyn lay on her back. Sheets covered her, but it appeared that her legs were drawn up with her knees wide apart. She was groaning and moving her body rhythmically. Her head and shoulders arched backward into the mattress. Carolyn's head turned slowly from side to side, moisture coming from the corner of her mouth. She was in the act of having sex with an invisible partner…sex she was enjoying and that was satisfying her. Ben stood shocked, mystified, and angry. He couldn't do anything, but watch.

Then, mixed with Carolyn's passion sounds, Ben heard laughter. It was Miller! Ben looked around the room for the antagonist. He wasn't visible. Ben ran to the bed and tore the sheets off of Carolyn expecting to see... what, he wasn't sure.

Instead of exposing her in the throes of
passion, he saw her body stretched out in a relaxed
position. Alone. Carolyn awoke with a start. She
looked up at him with shocked eyes that quickly
became angry. "What are you doing?" she demanded.

Ben looked at her and said what came into his
mind, "Did you have sex with Bill Miller?"

"You son-of-a-bitch!" Carolyn erupted like a
volcano. "How dare you! How dare you!" She threw
a pillow at him. "I've never. Can you say that, you
asshole!?" She pointed to the door. "Get out." When
he hesitated, she screamed, "Get... out!"

There was nothing to say. Ben headed for the
guest room for a night in a bed with his fears and
doubts his only company.

# # # # #

Chapter   23

"You awake in there?" Ben asked through the bedroom door. No answer.

"You okay?" No answer.

He rapped his knuckles on the wood making a loud thumping that should have awakened his light sleeping wife. "Carolyn, are you awake?"

Still, no answer.

"I need to get my clothes and stuff out to go to work." Carolyn didn't respond.

If Ben thought the sun would rise the next day and all his problems would evaporate like morning dew, he was shown early they would not. Carolyn wouldn't speak to him from behind her closed and locked door. He asked questions about her upcoming day, the children's schedules, and if she needed him to pick-up anything; she remained silent. He even tried a peace offering saying, "I'll go make coffee before I dress. I'll bring you a cup. What do you want in it?"

There was no response.

When Ben returned to the bedroom, coffee in hand, his clothes were hung on the locked doorknob. Everything else he needed was stacked on a tray on the hall floor. His knocks on the door and his attempts to talk through it were met with stony silence. Finally, exasperated, he beat his fists against the door and screamed, "We need to talk about this shit! You be in the kitchen in twenty minutes. I've got to get ready to go." Ben snatched his clothes and picked up the toiletry items, cursing as he retreated to the guest bathroom. While he showered, he heard Carolyn hustling the children off to school. His best effort to get out, dried, and partially dressed wasn't quick enough. Ben raced through the house in time to see Carolyn's car, with her and the children inside, pull out of the driveway.

* * *

Ben's day had started poorly and at work it got progressively worse. One of the large orders he was working on and felt was very secure, evaporated. The customer decided to postpone the purchase indefinitely. Since much of his pay check was based on commission, the loss hurt. A greater blow came from another account, one of Ben's steadiest customers since he started with the company. The buyer elected to go with a competitor and wouldn't tell Ben why. Even an offer for tickets to a Dolphins game landed on deaf ears.

Ben was still recovering from those two blows when the boss stuck his head into Ben's office. He smiled and said, "Good morning, Ben. Did you have a nice weekend? I saw you were out at the ranch. Catch any fish?"

"Oh yeah, plenty." Ben felt uncomfortable at any reminder of the terror he'd experienced, but forced a grin.

"Listen, I hate to spring this on you without warning, but I want you to stick around after work tonight for an important meeting. It's for the whole company. Can you make arrangements with Carolyn to come home late? It's going to take a while."

"Sure. Can you tell me what's going on?"

"Sorry, Ben. You'll have to wait because if I tell you I'll have to tell everyone. Hey, it isn't about you. Don't worry, it's not a bad thing."

"I guess I will just have to wait…patiently?" Ben said with an external smile and an internal frown. When the boss announced he was having a meeting after work, it historically brought major news of some sort—sometimes good, sometimes bad. He hoped the "not a bad thing" comment was true.

Ben wanted to find out what company intrigue was brewing and immediately devoted his morning to unmasking the mystery. He quickly found no one knew anything about the subject of the mysterious gathering. They were as curious as he was and as concerned. There were a few wild guesses, but no facts.

Ben hung around the executive office until it was empty. Then he tried his most reliable source, Myrtle, the boss's secretary, asking her, "Hey, sweetheart, what's going on? Ed told me we're having a big deal after work tonight. What can you tell me?"

"Not a thing. I don't know what's going on. Ed was closed up in his office a lot last week. You know that's not like him. He usually lets me in on everything, but not this time." She shrugged her shoulders, "I asked, but all he told me was that there wasn't anything for me to worry about."

"You have any guess on what it's about?"

"Not a clue. He's really kept whatever it is secret. I can tell you it's big. Everyone in the company except the most junior employees will have to attend. He had me send out an email to tell everyone coming to notify their families or others who might be waiting on them not to expect them home until late. The meeting is supposed to last until at least 7:00 PM." Myrtle sighed and smiled, "I think he's telling the truth about it not being bad. He's been very happy. You know, laughing and cutting up. When things are bad he's a real Scrooge."

Ben called Carolyn to tell her he'd be late for supper. He was relieved when she answered the phone rather than allowing the machine to take a message. Her response was cool, but he took her speaking to him at all as a thaw in the ice. She said, "There will be something you can heat up when you get home. The kids and I are going to go ahead and eat."

"Hey, I'm sorry about last night." His apology was met with stone cold silence.
Ben volunteered something he hadn't wanted to, "Look, maybe I should talk to the Doc. Maybe, I need some help. Maybe—"

Carolyn cut him off, saying, "This isn't something to discuss over the phone."

"Alright, I un—"

Carolyn ended the conversation by saying, "We will talk about this when you get home." She hung up without saying good-bye.

Late that afternoon, four strange men arrived at Ben's company. The boss and owner, Ed Hoffman, ushered the group into the executive offices and quickly closed the door. It was evident the men were to play some part in the evening's drama.

Ben made one final attempt to see if he could pry information from Myrtle. In the morning she'd been unconcerned and, Ben surmised, really didn't know what the meeting was about. When Ben saw her shortly before 5:00, she'd changed completely. Myrtle was nervous and her eyes twitched, her hazel pupils avoiding contact with his blue-gray ones. She told Ben she knew, but couldn't tell him, or anybody, anything. He would have to wait to find out.

When the meeting did begin, it didn't take long for everyone to learn its purpose. Within the first ten minutes, Ed announced he had decided to retire. He explained he'd sold the company to a large out-of-state firm who'd made "an offer I couldn't refuse." Ed introduced the four men Ben saw enter the office that afternoon. They were the "transition team." Within another fifteen minutes Ed turned the meeting over to one of the new company's representatives. The man told everyone to relax. No major changes were planned immediately. "Immediately?" His emphasis on that word was a fire alarm for every employee gathered there. He spent the next hour-and-a-half discussing the new company's policies, procedures, and personnel plans. The man's speech did little to lessen the shock and dismay on the faces of the staff and workers. Though everything sounded good, any change of the magnitude of the one being discussed was bound to be traumatic. Ben's world shook from another life-changing earthquake event.

After the meeting, Ben and a few fellow employees loitered in the office, talking about what the consequences were likely to be under the new ownership. Gloom and doom filled most predictions. One of the men said, "Well, I guess the sun will rise tomorrow. I'm going home before I make the little woman angry, too." Ben checked his watch; it was 8:30. He and three others were the only employees left in the office. Ben quickly excused himself; things were already tense enough between Carolyn and him. If it got much worse he might even have to go through with his promise to see the shrink. Coming in later in the evening wouldn't help.

# # # # #

Chapter 24

The day's whirlwind events had completely distracted him. It wasn't until Ben started across the parking lot that his other trouble pushed its way to the front of his mind. Dark. It was totally dark. The darkness brought the return of his most feared problem. When Ben took his first few steps on the parking lot blacktop, he felt the presence of his tormentor. Each stride intensified the feeling he was being stalked.

Halfway to his car he considered returning to the office. The urge to run back to the building intensified. He could stay all night; he'd done it before. Ben faked being there when he'd engaged in one of his affairs. But staying the night wasn't an option. That would definitely make Carolyn suspicious, madder, or both, than she already was. He began talking out loud to himself to buoy his courage. "It would be disastrous for me to be away from home given the problems Carolyn and I are having." He shook his head. "This is silly," Ben said it loudly, hoping to convince his mind it was acting irrational. The mound of dirt on its isolated prairie was far away. That's where the evil resided.

Ben took a couple more steps. The strange coldness he'd felt the previous night touched him, electrifying his being. Logic fled. Ben gave into his fear and he sprinted to his car, thanking God for the electronic door key. He vaulted up and into his SUV in a flash, slamming the door as quickly as he could.

Ben jammed his keys into the ignition, started the motor, and raced the engine as he slammed the car into gear. The tires squealed. Whatever lurked in the parking lot he'd soon leave far behind. When he swung the car around the empty lot toward the exit, he fully expected to see those two eyes peering at him, hating him. To his relief, nothing appeared. Ben shook his head. He told his mind his fears were totally baseless. "Shit, Ben you've got to get a grip," he mumbled to an empty back seat.

Ben wanted to get home fast. He pushed the speedometer ten miles over the speed limit, then fifteen, then twenty. He told himself he didn't want Carolyn stewing any longer than necessary. If at all possible he wanted the problems between them settled tonight. The other reason to get home quickly was the sanctuary it offered, though he refused to acknowledge that consciously. Two glowering balls of light were watching him, maybe even chasing the car, he was convinced of that. Ben couldn't drive into his garage soon enough.

Little or no traffic appeared to impede his progress. "Good, I'll be home in a half hour," Ben whispered. The sound of his voice soothed him. When Ben reached the well-lighted four-lane highway he felt safer. He had two miles to I-75, four more on the Interstate and another mile to his home.

"I don't need a ticket right now." Ben eased back on the accelerator. "Ten more minutes. That's all. I'll be home." Ben searched out the garage door opener, placed it next to him and hoped Carolyn's car wasn't blocking his entrance.

A half mile from the Interstate his feeling of safety abruptly disappeared. Coldness on the back of his neck made his hair stand up. A crawling sensation spread from shoulder to shoulder. Ben wanted to swat it away, but was afraid to…The spirit, the evil, was in the car with him. How in the hell can this be happening? He dismissed the thought, for that wasn't important. How wasn't critical; getting away from the nameless dread was. Getting home was. Ben focused on the road. He had to get into his house, quickly. His foot pushed the accelerator and the car zipped past seventy miles-per-hour. That would get him a ticket if a policeman saw him. "Good. A ticket and a cop would be welcome," Ben decided.

He increased his speed more. Ben approached the Interstate, knowing he'd have to make the turn onto the cloverleaf leading up to the expressway. To do that, he would have to change lanes and slow down. Ben glanced into the rearview mirror.

They were there! The eyes. Those two malevolent specters glared at him with their infinite, fierce hate. They were smaller and yet the same. Now only a couple inches in diameter they stared at him from a foot behind his backseat. The iris' colors were bright and flashing. Ben screamed, "Go away!"

He looked back at the road and told himself he would not look into the mirror again. As he aimed the car onto the cloverleaf ramp, the cold feeling spread forward on the sides of his head, over his ears. Suddenly, icy fingers pressed on his temples. Ben screamed, "God help me!" The pressure quickly increased and became vise-like. The fingertips pressed forward to the corner of his eyes, squeezing, the fingernails starting to dig in. Ben screamed, "No!" His hands left the steering wheel and Ben tried to pry the fingers away from his eyes. His foot slammed the accelerator to the floor. The cold pressure disappeared as he felt the car go airborne. Ben screamed a long continuous "Nooooooo!" Large pine trees filled his headlights. He heard the terrifying crunching of steel as he was slammed forward. The pine trees rushed at him...

# # # # #

Chapter 25

Blue, red, and yellow flashing lights illuminated the night creating a somber, silent scene. Two men stood by the mangled wreck that was Ben's SUV.

"How fast do you think he was going?"

"Seventy or maybe eighty." The highway patrolman shook his head. "Poor bastard never hit his brakes. No skid marks. He flew off the entrance ramp like a stunt car driver. He was probably sleeping or drunk."

The sheriff's deputy nodded. "He flew off it like a stunt driver, but that is as far as it goes. He didn't have his seat belt on. Maybe, suicide?" The deputy glanced at the distorted bloody car seat. "It's a good thing he had his wallet and license on him or he'd been a real project to identify."

"Did you see him?" the patrolman asked.

"I saw what was left of him." The deputy's face contorted. His expression told much. "Clayton and I helped the paramedics get him out. The med guys said he was dead the second he hit. His head was snapped backward and was at an angle I never saw before. One of them said he'd been yanking people out of wrecks for seventeen years and had never seen a body torn up worse. The other man agreed and puked thinking about it. They figured the rear view mirror tore through his face and on out the back of his skull. He didn't have his nose or eyes or anything. His face was a bloody pulp and missing from the mouth up. I'm not sure they ever found them, his eyes, I mean." The deputy shined his flashlight through the shattered windshield glass.

"Man. That's horrible. I'd hate to be the family member that has to I.D. the poor bastard." The patrolman looked through the smashed windshield and whistled. Blood was everywhere.

"It was the worst. Old Clayton took one look and heaved his cookies. He didn't stop hurling until the meat wagon took the corpse away. I've seen Clayton up to his elbows in deer guts and blood and eating a sandwich at the same time. I guess it's just different with humans." The deputy shook his head. "I told you even one of the med guys got queasy."

"How did you keep from getting sick?"

"I took one quick glance and didn't look at that part of him again. The face. The rest of him was bad enough. He was folded in there like an accordion." The deputy pointed at what was left of the SUV's driver's area. "There's only two or three feet between the dash and the seat. The legs were all broke up. Bloody. A real mess."

"Hey. Are you guys about done?" The wrecker driver ambled around the side of the SUV. "My dispatcher is on my ass to get this thing in and go to my next call."

"Yes," the patrolman answered. "It will just take a few minutes more." He nudged the deputy with his elbow. "Come help me stretch a tape so he can get this thing on the wrecker. I have to record how far I think it was airborne before it hit."

The two officers somberly walked to the exit ramp while the wrecker driver maneuvered his vehicle to remove the wasted vehicle much as the ambulance had when it removed the wasted life an hour before.

# # # # #

Epilogue

The sun lost its grip on the afternoon sky and slipped slowly to the western horizon. Its heat and light were dying just as Ben had the day before. The sun would rise again; Ben would not. The sand hill in the middle of the prairie remained, Ben did not.

On the mound, under its resident oaks, the only signs of human visitation were the campfire site and the shattered black radio, the only item forgotten in Ben and his family's haste to leave "a place no one should go." The late afternoon sun bathed the surrounding prairie in long shadows and silhouettes. Waning rays created diamonds of orange and purple on the creek's tiny wavelets. The spot's allure was constant…not dependent on man's presence to enjoy its splendor.

Walking the bank on the opposite side of the creek, a man's form approached. As the shadow neared, it was recognizable as the Indian. He stopped directly across from the campsite and looked at the mound on the other side. Only the trees could provide witness to what was about to happen. If anyone asked. If anyone cared. The Indian still wore the same clothes he had the first and last time Ben's family saw him.

As the sun dropped below the tree line, the Indian turned his back on the campsite and watched the orange globe until only its glow remained behind the oaks to the west. The sky's light blues darkened before he turned to look at the campsite again. The trees witnessed a subtle change in the Indian. His eyelids were pinched and sunken, covering vacant sockets. The facial features and coloring were no longer of any one race or ethnicity, but a mélange of every man. He extended his clenched fist and opened it palm upward. In that hand were two human eyes. Lifeless blue-gray pupils peeked through the sheen of their covering membranes. Had the evil the Calusa buried so long ago, reemerged? The form answered the question.

"I am in man's mind," the darkening specter roared for only the trees…the grass…the creatures…the wind to hear. The one who had been the Indian closed his fist on his newest prize. He stepped down into the creek and walked steadily into its depths until he disappeared beneath the dark waters.

A large water moccasin instantly appeared out of the water's depth at the point where the human form ceased to exist. It swam to the campsite shore and slithered out on the bank. In the last light of day, four recent but healing wounds behind the snake's head reflected pale white in contrast to its dark body. Evil had taken another form and returned to its second home, "A place no one should go."

THE END

DL Havlin
Author of Quality Fiction

DL Havlin is an eclectic author whose novels, novellas, and short stories mirror his rich, varied background. He has packed three lifetimes of experiences into one brim full existence. He believes, "The one big advantage writing at an advanced age provides is that life is what you know and not what you project it might be."

Schooled in Ft Myers, Florida, Anderson H.S., in Cincinnati, Ohio, and the University of Cincinnati, his widely varied career included: systems analyst, procedure writer, production manager, materials manager, licensed boat captain, fishing guide, high school football coach, product sales manager, manufacturing plant manager, worldwide divisional customer service director, chemicals distributor general manager, call center tech service rep, president and general manager of a small manufacturing company.

An avid lover of the outdoors and sports enthusiast, his passion for fishing, hunting and camping are frequently included in his writing. A deep love for nature and especially wild Florida often furnish settings for his work, but his travels make places such as Kiev, Singapore, London, New York, Modena, or Saxonhausen backgrounds for his stories as well.

His unique combination of a vivid imagination and his ability to weave intricate plot lines, seasoned by his life-time exposure to fascinating story possibilities and his knowledge of human nature, provides the heart-felt, enjoyable reading his novels provide.

He answers, "Why do you write?" by saying, "To entertain— that's first, but to provoke thought is a close second. I firmly believe both are done through the heart, for the mind is seldom opened until it is emotionally conditioned to respond."

www.ingramcontent.com/pod-product-compliance
Lightning Source LLC
Chambersburg PA
CBHW070511260626
47161CB00004B/1513